Kim took a deep breath and flopped down on the easy chair.

"Look, Carrie," Kim said gently, "you have to take a few risks in life. You already told me that you never knew what it was like to have a gang of friends. This is your opportunity to change all of that."

"Maybe. Why do you think so?"

"I get the impression the S.N. members really stick together, and they wouldn't be asking us if they didn't think we would fit in."

"They haven't asked us officially. Renée said she'd be back in two days to talk some more. Is that what she said to you?"

"Renée told me she'd be here day after tomorrow, same time, same place," Kim answered honestly. Then she quickly added, "I think it'll be so much fun. I can't see any reason not to join."

"Then I'll say yes. As you say, I have to learn to take risks."

THE CLUB

Patricia Aks

FAWCETT JUNIPER • NEW YORK

RLI: $\dfrac{\text{VL: 6 \& up}}{\text{IL: 7 \& up}}$

A Fawcett Juniper Book
Published by Ballantine Books

Copyright © 1987 by Patricia Aks

Library of Congress Catalog Card Number: 87-91009

ISBN 0-449-70238-3

Manufactured in the United States of America

First Edition: February 1988

Chapter 1

*C*arrie Gordon, lugging a heavy suitcase, managed to find the double room she'd been assigned on the third floor of Ellsworth without asking anyone for directions. In fact, she'd been able to travel all the way from Butler, Kansas, to the Adams School in Chestervale, Virginia, without exchanging two words with anyone. It was a matter of pride for Carrie to be self-sufficient—independent to the point that she might appear standoffish. Ever since her mother died, five years ago, Carrie had determined to take care of herself, and her way of doing so was to act as though she didn't need anyone.

Room 301 was at the end of a long hall, and Carrie was gratefully surprised at its spaciousness. It easily accommodated two of everything—beds, dressers, desks, chairs—and had two large windows that overlooked the campus. A long oblong table in the center divided the room so that each girl's area was clearly defined.

Carrie heaved a sigh of relief—the living arrangement was the next best thing to having a single. She was an only child and so accustomed to privacy that sharing a room with someone she hadn't even met added to her apprehensions about going to boarding school.

She was pleased to see that the trunk she'd sent ahead had arrived safely, and although she was tired from the three-hour flight and the emotional exhaustion of saying good-bye to her father, she began unpacking. After she had unloaded everything and put her belongings away, she made her bed and collapsed on it.

Carrie had been so preoccupied with getting settled in her part of the room that she hadn't looked too carefully at her roommate's half. Now she glanced across, and felt a combination of despair and amusement. The school had notified her that her roommate's name was Ginger Ambrose, and Carrie had thought about her all during the flight, fantasizing that they would have a lot in common. She hoped Ginger would be a serious student, like long-hair music, consider it a privilege to go to Adams. But the evidence was just the opposite.

The most obvious thing about Ginger was that she was into horses. A large poster of a horse standing in a meadow leaned against her desk; two richly waxed pairs of boots, one deep brown and the other cordovan, stood in front of the unmade bed; a riding whip hung from the doorknob; a black velvet riding helmet, the kind Carrie had only seen in glossy fashion magazines, was perched on the desk lamp; and an honest-to-goodness saddle burnished to a lustrous sheen was on the floor.

Carrie had promised herself that she wouldn't make snap judgments about anyone, but it was clear that Ginger wasn't exactly neat, the tapes carelessly piled on her desk were anything but "classical," and the most serious book on her shelf was entitled *Thoroughbreds: An Illustrated History of Racehorses*. From the looks of her closet, spilling over with clothes, she was undoubtedly rich. Carrie wondered if the computer that had been programmed to pick roommates had gone tilt or been invaded by gremlins. She didn't know whether to laugh or cry, and bit her lip in order to avoid doing either, when a hundred-pound blue-jeaned girl with curly red hair streaked into the room.

"Hi, I'm Ginger," she exclaimed, and radared a smile so bright that Carrie momentarily stopped worrying about computer errors. "You must be Carrie."

"That's right," Carrie answered, and started to stand up.

"Don't move," Ginger said. "I know you came all the way from Kansas, and you must be wiped out. I arrived this morning from Richmond—my parents drove me to make sure I got here. It's the last place I want to be, but they think I need discipline and Adams is the place." She straddled her desk chair and her brown eyes twinkled as she observed Carrie's five-foot-eight frame, her pale complexion, and her nondescript hair. Then she squinted at the books, mostly science tomes plus the complete works of Shakespeare, that were precisely lined up on the shelf above Carrie's bare desk. Still smiling, she sighed wearily.

"What's wrong?" Carrie asked nervously.

"Nothing, except I think the housing dean must believe that opposites attract, or maybe my mother told her to put me in with an intellectual neatnik."

"I'm not that," Carrie protested.

"I didn't mean that the way it sounded," Ginger apologized. "One thing you'll have to get used to about me is that I always say what's on my mind. Actually, as you might have guessed, the only thing I care about is horses, and I'd like to major in them. I'm a fast learner, so I'll manage to pass all the courses, but I couldn't care less about school. What about you?"

"I care a lot, especially about science. I want to be a doctor. And you?"

"I want to be a jockey."

Carrie looked so dismayed that Ginger quickly added, "Only kidding. Anyhow, I'm really easy to get along with, especially since we've got our own turf. I promise not to interfere with your studying. I've got two friends down the hall and they're just about as big goof-offs as I am, so I'll play my music in their room. I'm going to bring my tapes over right now." Ginger bounced out of her chair.

"You can play them here, and maybe you'd like to hear some of the tapes I brought—mostly Brahms, Bach, and Beethoven."

"Thanks a lot, but no thanks," Ginger said. She piled up the tapes on her desk and headed for the door. "Really nice meeting you, Carrie, and good luck."

"Same to you," Carrie answered.

Carrie felt a sinking feeling in the pit of her stomach. Ginger was nice, but they had absolutely nothing in common. The closest Carrie had come to horseback riding was when she was eight years old and had been walked around on a pony at the local fair. And Ginger didn't seem the least bit inclined to share any of her interests. Well, Carrie thought philosophically, I wanted a single room, and I think this might as well be one.

Carrie felt a little foolish when she suddenly realized that she was still in her navy blue traveling suit and matching shoes. The last thing she wanted to look like was weird, and Ginger's words "intellectual neatnik" still stung. She kicked off her shoes, stood up, and started to take off her jacket, when there was a loud knocking on the partly opened door. A large blond girl with a resonant voice said, "Can I come in?" and entered the room before Carrie could say anything.

4

"I'm Ellen Giles, president of the house, and I thought we ought to get to know each other."

"Sure," Carrie said, "I'm Carrie Gorden."

"I would like everyone in our house to meet in the lounge, and I've taken it on myself to round up the new arrivals. There're about ten new girls, and since we don't want you wandering around like lost sheep, some of us experienced Ellsworthians thought we could show you the ropes. Mrs. Gore is our housemother, and she'll be there. She's about as effective as a snowball in summer, but harmless. Then we thought we'd show you around the campus. Be downstairs in twelve minutes, okay?" It was more a statement than a question.

"Sure," Carrie answered, and wondered what would have happened if she'd refused.

"See you in twelve minutes," Ellen said, and left the room as abruptly as she had entered.

Carrie quickly changed into a straight beige skirt, a white camp shirt, and loafers. She always dressed conservatively, never wanting to draw attention to herself. Then she made her way down the corridor, aware as she passed the rooms along the way that the atmosphere was charged with excitement. There was a steady stream of chatter, occasional exclamations of delight, and peals of laughter. By contrast, Carrie felt out of it. Everyone seemed to know everyone, and as she descended the stairs, a couple of girls brushed past her, muttering, "Scuse us," as though she were a stranger entering a subway.

The lounge was furnished comfortably with sofas, love seats, and floor pillows, all covered in earth tones of gold, rust, and green. There was a scattering of pull-up chairs, and Carrie sat down on one in the back of the room and looked around. Ginger was sprawled on a floor pillow at the opposite end, babbling nonstop to two girls next to her, probably the goof-offs. Then she spotted Carrie, waved, and went right on talking.

There were ten new students in Ellsworth, and it baffled Carrie that everyone seemed to be old friends. Would she always be a loner? she wondered.

"Attention, everyone." Ellen had closed the door to the lounge and stood in front of it. She spoke in a crisp voice that immediately quieted the group. "I want to welcome the new girls to our house, Ellsworth, which happens to be the best on the campus. There's no point in being modest— we've got the best students, the best athletes, and the greatest spirit. The other houses have their share of jocks and brains, but they can't compare to Ellsworth. If you don't believe me, just ask any Ellsworthian."

There was a sprinkling of laughter, and a couple of girls shouted, "She's right!" "We're the greatest!" "Incomparable!"

"We've also got an exceptional housemother, Mrs. Gore, and she'd like to say something. Then I'll get back to you."

Carrie thought, What a clever description. *Exceptional* could mean anything, and as Mrs. Gore spoke a few words, she was sure "exceptionally boring but nice" might be a more accurate description.

Mrs. Gore was a small birdlike woman who fluttered as she talked. "I want everyone to be happy," she began, "so please don't break the rules, because it hurts me to have to report anyone to our headmistress, Mrs. Gladstone. One thing I've learned in my six years as housemother is that you girls are very careless about signing out. That's something you must do, just by putting your name, the hour of your departure, and your destination on the checkout sheet posted on the bulletin board in the front hall. Not checking out is a no-no, and when it happens and I can't find one of my girls, I get so upset."

There were a few snickers from the audience, but Mrs. Gore went right on. "The main thing I want to say is that I'm here whenever you need me. My suite is on this floor, across the hall from the lounge. Now, I won't keep you any longer, because I know that Ellen has planned a tour for the new girls. I wish you all the best of luck."

Everyone applauded, and once again Ellen took over the meeting. "We've only got forty minutes until supper, so we should get started right away. We'll assemble outside in five minutes and wind up at the dining hall so you don't have to return to the dorm."

The ten new girls appeared promptly in front of Ellsworth, and Ellen introduced them to two upperclasswomen. "This is Sally and Amy, who are seniors, and between the three of us we can answer any questions. I think the best place to get a view of the school is from 'the dimple.'" She then led the way down a gentle grass-covered slope in the center of the campus.

"As you can see, all the buildings surround this one stretch of lawn. Beyond them is the orchard."

"Great place for a picnic," someone remarked.

"Forget it," said Ellen. "The groundskeeper, Mr. Armstrong, takes it personally if one blade of grass is destroyed. Some kids were tossing a Frisbee out here one day last spring. He happened to see them and boomed through his megaphone that the 'nature violators' better find another place to play. None of us like to cross Mr. Armstrong."

For the next half hour the girls trooped past the other dorms, Franklin, Andrews, and Madison; saw the music, science, and administration buildings, the gym and library, and the imposing house of the headmistress. The architecture was consistently Southern antebellum, with white pillars and red brick walls.

After that, they strolled toward the hockey field and

tennis courts, and then to the stables. As they approached, Carrie found herself standing next to Ginger and her friends. Ginger promptly introduced Suzy and Lisa, who were just as smiley as Ginger, and chattered about horses as though they were people. They were polite, but so absorbed in comparing the merits of the horses they rode at home to the ones at school that Carrie was soon excluded from the conversation.

"That's Maximilian, my favorite so far," said Suzy, a short apple-cheeked brunette, pointing to a strawberry roan.

"Not good with my coloring," Ginger said, giggling.

"Maybe that's why I'm always partial to chestnut horses," Lisa commented. "Brings out the highlights in my blond hair better than any rinse." Then the three of them cracked up, and moved off, forgetting all about Carrie.

When they had traipsed through the stable, a tall, willowy blonde said, "Horses are great, but where are the boys?"

"Across the lake," Ellen said. "The boys' school is off-limits weekdays, unless there's an official reason for going there. But we'll go to the lake now, and you can see where we do our water sports."

"You mean the only way to get to the boys' school is to swim?" Ginger piped up.

"There's a dirt road that runs around the lake, so you don't have to get wet to get there."

"How long does it take?"

"I think eight minutes is the record."

When they arrived at the lake and edged toward the end of the dock, it was possible to see the boys' pier and boathouse opposite. The campus was hidden from view by the trees, and the willowy blonde quipped, "So near and yet so far."

"Don't worry," Ellen said, "there really are boys there.

Now we better make tracks to the dining hall. Since this is your first meal, they'll probably spring for creamed chicken. That's their company dish."

There was a collective groan, but then the girls picked up their pace and chatted animatedly as they followed Ellen. Carrie overheard snatches of conversation that made her feel more and more like an outsider. There was talk of deb parties, skiing holidays, tropical vacations. When she stood in line cafeteria-style for what sure enough was creamed chicken, and sat down at one of the large round tables that seated eight, the talk about a world totally alien to Carrie continued. She knew it couldn't be true, but for the moment she felt she must be the only scholarship student at Adams.

Chapter 2

That night as they were getting ready for bed, Ginger said that she planned to skip assembly.

"Nobody will know, and you can tell me what happened."

"Ginger, it's our first official day of school, and the Book of Rules says we're on the honor system. Besides, don't you want to see what Mrs. Gladstone is like?"

"I guess so."

"Besides, it only meets once a week."

"I know, but I have trouble getting up in the morning."

"I'll make sure you do."

"I can see I'm living with a Girl Scout," Ginger said, but she smiled so disarmingly that Carrie didn't take offense.

Carrie had set her alarm for seven-thirty. She leapt out of bed as soon as it went off, put on a robe and slippers, grabbed a towel and washcloth, and then hurried to the community bathroom to wash up. When she returned to the room, Ginger was still sound asleep.

Carrie urged her in a soft voice to wake up, and then finally resorted to gently shaking her.

"Where am I?" Ginger mumbled, rubbing her eyes.

"You're at school, and we have exactly twenty-three minutes to make it to assembly."

"Oh yeah," Ginger said, and dragged herself out of bed. Then she padded barefoot down the hall, and returned in less than five minutes, blotting her face dry.

"Thank goodness this happens only once a week." Ginger still sounded groggy and started to pull on the jeans she had carelessly tossed on a chair the night before.

"Those aren't allowed," Carrie said, glancing up as she smoothed the sheets on her bed.

"Huh?"

"The dress code, remember? 'Jeans are not permitted except on Sunday.' "

"You are so right," Ginger sighed. "I did read the Book of Rules, but so long ago that I've conveniently forgotten most of them."

She stepped out of the jeans, leaving them where they fell, and pulled a green skirt and a blouse printed with tiny horses out of her closet. She was slipping the blouse over her head when Suzy appeared at the door.

"You ready, Ginger?" she asked.

"Almost."

"Lisa and I will go ahead and save you a seat in the back. That's the best place to be in case we nod off." She started to walk away, stopped suddenly, and added, "We'll save one for you too, Carrie."

"Thanks," Carrie said, knowing she was only an afterthought. She would have preferred sitting up close, to make sure she didn't miss anything, but she was too polite to say so.

As it turned out, the acoustics in the auditorium were excellent.

Mrs. Gladstone could be heard in every corner of the assembly hall. Until she spoke, she seemed like a sweet lavender-and-lace, old-fashioned grandmother. Her gray hair, her eyes bespectacled in wire-framed granny glasses, the soft mauve suit, pale pink blouse, and sensible shoes she was wearing enhanced her grandmotherly appearance. But her clear, strong voice belied her demure impression, and the words she spoke extolling the value of an Adams education were inspiring.

Carrie was genuinely moved by her speech and applauded enthusiastically when Mrs. Gladstone finished with the words, "It behooves all of us to take to heart our school motto: 'Enter to learn, go forth to serve.'"

Lisa, who Carrie had already learned was more apt to be sarcastic than accurate, remarked, "The only thing I'd like to learn is what's for breakfast, and when it will be served."

Ginger and Suzy giggled appreciatively as the audience got up from their seats and started to leave. Carrie wasn't in the mood for treating the headmistress's speech so lightly. She managed to lose Ginger and her friends in the crowd, even though it meant sitting for breakfast with some kids she didn't know at all.

Carrie went through the cafeteria line and helped herself to cornflakes, a carton of milk, tea, and a blueberry muffin. She balanced her tray in front of her as she weaved her way among the tables, looking for an empty place. She was so intent in scanning the dining room that she didn't notice someone pushing back her chair, which jostled Carrie's arm and sent everything on her tray flying. Carrie was mortified, but the girl—a vivacious-looking brunette—kept saying, "My fault, my fault," grabbed a bunch of paper napkins from the container on the table, and started mopping up.

Everyone at the table was laughing, and one girl said, "We can't take you any place, Kim."

"That's what everyone says," Kim said good-naturedly as she ducked under the table to retrieve the blueberry muffin. Then she jumped up and dumped the whole mess into one of the trash cans strategically placed in the corners of the room.

Carrie called after her, "Thanks a lot."

"No problem," Kim said, and waved her hand.

Carrie returned to the food counter and once again helped herself to tea and a muffin. Still feeling embarrassed, she headed away as far as possible from Kim's table and finally settled down with a group of three girls who were getting ready to leave. They looked like seniors.

"We're going back to the dorm before classes," one of them explained. "Each of us managed to forget something."

"After three years here, you'd think we'd be prepared," another one said.

"Must be psychological," the third added.

Then they all stood up, slid their trays off the table, and headed for the stacking rack.

Carrie felt a little self-conscious sitting alone, but it gave her a chance to pull herself together. Her father, Len, had warned her that being away from home for the first time can be very difficult, and so far she had to agree. Then she remembered his words as he gave her a final hug before she boarded the plane: "You know our family comes from pioneer stock, and we've always been able to conquer new frontiers."

Carrie knew he'd been half kidding. Len always made her laugh by exaggerating her fears, starting when she was six years old and insisted on sleeping with her door open. Instead of giving her an argument, he told her it was a good idea. "You never know when a grizzly bear might wander into the house." Even at that early age, he managed to make her laugh at herself.

She'd been at Adams only two days, and it seemed like a hundred. She believed she was the only "pioneer" who never rode a horse, and who made her entrance into a dining hall by tripping over a chair and dropping her tray. It was not a beginning marked by success, she thought as she finished her tea. But then she wasn't here for fun and games, she was here to study, and that's what she really cared about . . . wasn't it?

Before she could answer her own question, the bell clanged, which meant breakfast was over and classes were to begin in ten minutes. Carrie stacked her tray, and then headed for the main building, Room 201, pleased that her first class was in American literature. If the teacher was good, Carrie was sure she'd stop worrying about her personal problems.

Carrie was one of the first girls to arrive in the classroom and took a seat in one of the middle rows. She didn't want to appear too eager by sitting up front. Slowly the room was filled, and when the final bell rang, the teacher strode in. He was a short, round, middle-aged man whose most distinctive feature was his eyes, which twinkled under shaggy eyebrows. In spite of his stature, he was imposing.

"Good morning, young ladies. As you may have learned, if you bothered to read the catalog, I'm Mr. Benson and this is a course in American literature. I know you are the television generation, and my sole ambition is to turn you on to books. I believe you'll find the reading fascinating if you don't resist it. Also, you'll find I'm a very lenient teacher . . . provided you do exactly what's required."

There was a ripple of laughter and Mr. Benson continued.

"Please raise your hand and stand up when I call your name. This is known as taking attendance and it's also my way of getting to know you."

There were fifteen girls in the class, and some of them looked vaguely familiar to Carrie. The one who caught her attention was Kim, whose last name she learned was Miller. Kim was memorable to Carrie not just because of their encounter in the dining room but also because she had a charismatic quality—a green-eyed pixie look that was irresistible.

Kim was a few seats away in Carrie's row, and she caught Carrie's eye as she stood up when her name was called. Then, when Mr. Benson's head was bent over his list, and before she started to sit down, Kim whispered, "You vanished!"

Carrie just shrugged her shoulders and thought maybe she had overreacted. After all, what was so terrible about spilling a little food?

After attendance was taken, Mr. Benson gave a brief description of the first semester's work.

"We'll be reading Hemingway first, starting with *A Farewell to Arms*, a book that embodies in its main character Hemingway's code. The hero, Frederic Henry, sees life simply. He is not afraid of death and prefers physical pleasures to intellectual pursuits . . . perhaps like members of this class. By the way, have any of you read this book?"

Kim's hand shot up, and Carrie tentatively started to raise hers. Mr. Benson looked at Kim, obviously not noticing Carrie. "You're lucky. I've read it at least ten times and each time I see something new. I guarantee you will, too."

"I know I will," Kim said. "I was in sixth grade when I read it, and I didn't know *anything* about life then."

The whole class laughed, and even Mr. Benson grinned. Then he told how the book was a story of love and war, and he listed a number of questions that the reader should keep in mind, including the meaning of the title. By the time the bell rang, everyone's interest had been piqued, and Carrie knew she had lucked out in getting into Mr. Benson's course.

There was a ten-minute break between classes, and Carrie had already decided to go to the bookstore, which was downstairs in the same building, before going to her next class. She rushed out and was halfway down the hall when Kim caught up with her.

"Hey, are you avoiding me?" she asked breathlessly.

Carrie slowed down and then seeing the humor in the situation burst out laughing. "Not really," she answered. "To tell the truth, I was so embarrassed in the dining hall that I would have happily gone through the floor." Carrie was surprised herself that she could admit anything so stupid to a complete stranger, but there was something about Kim. . . .

"That's crazy. I'm the one that should have been embarrassed, and it didn't bother me at all."

"I noticed," Carrie said wistfully.

In order to avoid the stampede of kids coming out of the classrooms, the two girls moved away from the center of the corridor and leaned against the wall.

"The other thing I want to know is why you didn't say you'd read Hemingway? I saw your hand go up, sort of. . . ."

"Don't know."

"I wish you had. Not that there's any danger of me being accused of being a brain, but I don't like being a show-off. Anyhow, where and what's your next class?"

"It's French, and it's in this building."

"Then why the hurry?"

"I thought I'd buy *A Farewell to Arms* in the bookstore before they're all sold out."

"Don't worry about that. I brought my copy from home, and you can always borrow it."

"That's good to know. Actually, I'm trying to build up my library, and as long as it's in paperback I can afford it."

Kim was astounded. "You're the first person I've met, besides me, who's worried about affording something."

"Well, I do get an allowance, but I have to be careful. I'm on a scholarship so I don't . . ."

"You are? Me too," Kim said gleefully. "I thought I was the only one in the entire school who wasn't homesick for her horse."

Carrie chuckled. "I know what you mean."

Kim glanced at her watch. "Look, my biology class is in the science building, and if I don't fly there this second I'll be late. When can we continue this conversation?"

"I'm in Ellsworth, 301."

"And I'm 324—the opposite end. Will you be in your room after classes, about four o'clock?"

"Absolutely."

"Terrific. I've met a lot of kids and they're all friendly, but I think you and I might be soul mates," Kim said laughing and raced down the hall without waiting for a response.

Carrie watched until she disappeared down the stairs, and smiled. Kim's enthusiasm was contagious, and even though Carrie knew she was exaggerating about being soul mates, she felt a warm glow at the thought that she had found a friend.

Chapter 3

*C*arrie had been tempted on at least six different occasions to telephone her father. She resisted, not just because of the expense of a long-distance call but also because she didn't want him to get the idea that she was homesick. It would have been impossible to hide her feelings, and therefore she kept putting it off. With each succeeding day, the homesickness diminished, and then she decided to write him a letter.

Dear Daddy,
I can't believe ten days have passed since I left Butler. If time continues to go so fast, I'll be home for Thanksgiving before you know it.
My courses are great, especially biology and American lit. In bio, we have real frogs to dissect. Did you know how closely their insides resemble ours? And next semester we'll be working on fetal pigs. I can't wait! You were right about Adams having state-of-the-art lab equipment—something I could never have at Butler High.

My roommate's name is Ginger and we both laugh at how crazy it is that we were assigned the same room. She couldn't care less about school and has no intention of going to college. Even though she's smart, she's convinced she wouldn't have been accepted if her father hadn't been an alum. Her ambition in life is to get married and raise horses—not necessarily in that order. The good thing about Ginger is that she has a good sense of humor, and tells me she's doing me a favor by spending all her free time in the stables, which gives me the room to myself.

Yesterday I tried out for orchestra and made it! All those flute lessons paid off. Actually, theater, orchestra, and chorus are the only activities we share with the boys' school, and they take place on their campus in the music building. I think I'm one of the few kids who didn't try out for just that reason.

I haven't made a lot of friends, but there's one girl, Kim Miller, who I really like. She happens to be on a full scholarship too, comes from Woodvale, a small suburb of Philadelphia, has a younger brother and sister. Her mom works part-time as a substitute teacher and her father has a job in the post office. We decided that every other kid's father at Adams is a banker or a lawyer or an executive in a big corporation. Kim says her father doesn't own the post office, and I told her you taught math in a junior college and weren't president. That made us tighter than ever.

Now I can tell you that the first few days were really bumpy. But things get better all the time and I can honestly say I'm glad I'm here. I miss you a lot and hope you have a collection of students who know their sums!

> *Loads of love,*
> *Carrie*

Carrie reread the letter and addressed the envelope, pleased that she was able to tell the truth. Things were getting better all the time. She wished she'd been able to say she'd made a lot of new friends, because that would have made her father really happy. One of the reasons he wanted her to go on to boarding school was so she would branch out. That might never happen, but for the first time in her life she'd met someone who was fast becoming her best friend.

One of the first things Kim noticed when she dropped by 301 was how neat Carrie's half of the room always was. On one of her visits after supper, when Ginger was out of the room, she asked her about it.

"I'm used to keeping it that way, I guess. I don't have anyone to pick up after me." Carrie pushed back her chair from her desk and turned to face Kim, who flopped down on the bed.

"You must be your mother's dream." Kim laughed.

"I don't have a mother."

"You what?" Kim was stunned.

"My mother died when I was nine."

"I can't believe it. I can't imagine not having my mother. I mean . . . I mean . . . what's it like?"

"No one ever asked me that before. I guess that's because the people I grew up with saw it happening. My mother was sick on and off for a year, and then it was all over."

"Maybe you don't want to talk about it."

"I don't mind. I miss her, and I always will, but my father and I have managed. We're really close—we needed each other, maybe too much."

"And that's why you came to Adams."

"That's one of the reasons. Right after my mother died, my father got a lot of invitations from his friends, but he refused them because he didn't want to leave me with a babysitter. Then we got into this routine of having a pizza and going to a movie every Friday night. He always wanted me to bring a classmate along, but I didn't want to share him with anyone." Carrie shrugged her shoulders helplessly.

"I can see why in the beginning, but when you got older . . ."

"Things didn't change."

"Didn't you go to parties? In Woodvale, we live for parties."

"I did go, but they weren't terrific. I mean being five foot eight I felt like I towered over all the boys—sort of like the *Queen Mary* being escorted by a bevy of tugboats."

Kim giggled at the image. "That's a great height, perfect for clothes, and you're pretty besides. You could be a model."

Carrie laughed out loud. "Me? A model? You must be kidding. I couldn't care less about clothes."

"Thought so," Kim muttered under her breath, and quickly added, "I'm five three, and would love to be at least three inches taller."

"And you do care about clothes."

Kim nodded her head vigorously. "And parties, and boys. For those reasons Woodvale is the greatest."

"Then why go to boarding school?"

"It was all because of Mrs. Talley. She's the principal of our school, happens to be an Adams graduate, and also is a friend of my parents. For that reason, she took a special interest in me. And . . ." Kim hesitated.

"And you're smart, right?"

Kim giggled. "You're a mind reader. I'm not what you'd call a workaholic, but I did score high on the end-of-the-year intelligence tests. That gave Talley the opportunity she'd been looking for. She convinced my parents, and me, that I needed more challenges than Woodvale could offer. I hated to leave my family and friends, but once I got the scholarship, I couldn't see turning it down. And much to my amazement, I think it's going to be fine."

"Me too," Carrie said, thinking that just talking to Kim

helped her shed many of her misgivings about boarding school.

Kim stayed until the Lights Out warning bell sounded, and they could have gone on for hours. After that, Kim and Carrie had a rap session almost every night. Sometimes, especially when it was in Kim's room, other girls would drift in. Carrie knew that Kim made friends easily, and that she didn't, but she was beginning to feel less like an outsider. Also, she wasn't threatened by Kim's friends because she knew she had more in commom with Kim than any of the other girls, including her roommate, Nancy.

Nancy Green was a short, slightly plump, angel-faced, curly-headed blonde who spent most of her free time writing letters to her boyfriend back home. She revealed at one of the rap sessions that her parents had sent her to Adams because they thought she was too young to be so serious about a boy.

"My father, who treats me as though I'm a member of his organization, goes, 'You'll get some perspective if you're away from Sam. He's a very nice boy, but you shouldn't cut off your options.'"

"Is he right?"

"Yes, he's right that I've got some perspective—I like Sam better than ever. He's so cute and funny and . . ."

She stopped in mid-sentence when she noticed that Kim was trying not to giggle. "I know," Nancy went on. "I'm really boring. But that's what being in love means. Anyhow, Carrie, what about you? Do you have a boyfriend?"

Carrie shook her head. "Nope. Never had and don't now. I've liked a few boys, but not that way."

"You don't know what you're missing, right, Kim?"

"Right," Kim agreed. "I believe in boyfriends—especially in vast numbers."

"I'll settle for just one," Nancy said dreamily. Then she

glanced at her watch. "Speaking of which, it's time for my nine o'clock call."

She leapt up from the bed where she had been lying, grabbed a change purse that was sitting on her desk, and explained to Carrie, "This is my night to phone. We take turns."

"If your father knew how much you were paying Ma Bell, he might reconsider sending you away," Kim joked, as Nancy left the room.

Kim was on the floor, in the lotus position, and looked for a response from Carrie. Carrie, who was sprawled sideways on the easy chair, her legs flung over the arm, smiled briefly, and then her eyes clouded.

"What are you thinking?" Kim asked.

Carrie didn't say anything for the longest time.

"Too heavy to talk about," Kim said.

"Sort of," Carrie answered.

"Things get lighter when you talk about them." Kim put her hands over her head and stretched to one side and then the other.

"Well," Carrie said after another long pause, "I'm wondering if I'll ever have a boyfriend."

Kim stopped exercising and put her hands on her hips. "Of course you will! You're a perfectly red-blooded American girl in her formative years."

"So why don't I?"

"Because, for whatever reason, you weren't ready. Now you are, and now you'll find one. Who knows, maybe at this very moment someone across the lake is sitting in his room, pining for a statuesque girl from Butler, Kansas, who doesn't . . ." Kim suddenly stopped talking and looked slightly embarrassed.

"Doesn't what?" Carrie put her feet down and sat straight up in the chair.

"Never mind."

"Come on, Kim."

Kim still hesitated.

"Say it," Carrie insisted. "You're my friend, aren't you?"

"I am," Kim said firmly. "And I will say it. You . . . you don't have your antennae out."

"You mean like this?" Carrie put her fists on either side of her head and wiggled her fingers.

Then the two of them got a case of the giggles.

"That's not exactly what I mean," Kim said, trying to be serious again. "What I mean is, you've got classic features, and really nice coppery-colored hair, and you're tall and thin, and . . . and you don't do anything with any of it. Why?"

Carrie looked thoughtful. "You really want to know?"

"Sure I do."

"You promise not to laugh?"

"Cross my heart."

"I always thought I was kind of plain-looking, my hair neither dark or light, and I'm built like an ironing board. I don't want to bring attention to myself."

"That is the most ridiculous thing I ever heard! I thought you were smart!"

Carrie looked crestfallen, and Kim realized she'd hurt her feelings. "I'm sorry," Kim said. "I just can't believe you have such a bad image of yourself. I guess that's why you never volunteer in class, although I notice when you're called on, you always have the answers. And when Benson gave us that little surprise quiz last week—'Write for ten minutes on Hemingway's attitude toward women, based on his portrayal of Catherine'—it was your paper he read aloud."

"That's true, but it doesn't solve my antenna problem."

It was obvious that Carrie was trying hard to be honest with herself. "What should I do?" she said in a soft voice.

Kim was aware that Carrie really did want advice, that even though she had a loving father, there were things she couldn't talk to him about. And she had indicated that she'd never been close to anyone else. Carrie's mother's sister, Mary, lived two hundred miles away with her husband, Ken, and their two little sons. Aunt Mary was great, Carrie had told her, but because of the distance they rarely got together. Kim was reminded of how many times a day she asked her mother the dumbest questions, and again she was overwhelmed with a wave of sympathy that she tried not to show to her new friend.

"Well," Kim began, choosing her words carefully, "you would look terrific in colors. Whenever I've got the blahs, I put on something wild and I feel a lot better. I don't think I've ever seen you in anything but gray and beige and navy blue. Not that you don't look nice, but . . ."

"But dullsville," Carrie chimed in.

Kim chuckled. "You said it, I didn't."

"They are practical, though. I can mix them up, and everything matches."

"Who wants to be practical?" Kim jumped up, ran to her chest of drawers, and pulled out a soft lipstick-red cardigan.

"This is my absolutely favorite sweater. I save it for special occasions. I think it has magical powers because every time I wear it something good happens. Try it on and see how you look." Kim presented the sweater to Carrie with a low bow.

Carrie slipped it on, and then viewed herself in the full-length mirror on the closet door. "It's beautiful, but I look so pale."

"We can do something about that," Kim said gleefully.

She opened the top drawer of her dresser, took out two fistfuls of cosmetics, and dumped them on her desk.

"It looks like you're planning to open a makeup store," Carrie said, goggle-eyed. "All I own is a Chap Stick."

Kim shook her head despairingly and bit her tongue before she said something insulting, like "That's obvious."

"Nancy gave me these," she explained. "Her father is a director in a cosmetic firm and gets zillions of samples. You can take whatever you want."

"I wouldn't know what to do with them."

"Sit down, madam, and I'll show you." Kim guided her to her desk chair with a flourish and handed her a large mirror. "This will be your first makeup lesson."

Carrie stiffened, not used to this kind of attention.

"Relax," Kim ordered. "This is not like going to the dentist!"

Carrie leaned back and laughed, breaking the tension. For the next fifteen minutes, Kim kept up a running monologue as she showed Carrie how to apply makeup. "With eye shadow, it should be darker on the lids, lighter near the brow." "Blush should emphasize the cheekbones, and work down." "Go easy on the lipstick, just a touch of color so you look alive."

"*Voilà!*" Kim exclaimed when she finished. "*Magnifique!*" "*Trés jolie!*"

Carrie couldn't stop staring at her image in the mirror and smiling. "I like it," she said, "I like it."

"And now the sweater looks terrific on you."

Carrie, with uncharacteristic boldness, said, "I know it, I know it."

Just at that moment Nancy ambled into the room, smiling to herself as she repeated in her head all the romantic things Sam had said to her. She sat down at her desk and gazed at his silver-framed eight-by-ten photo.

Ordinarily, Kim was too tactful to interrupt her roommate's trance, but tonight was different. Kim coughed loudly and rasped "Ahem" several times.

"You trying to tell me something?" Nancy murmured, still preoccupied.

"Yes!" Kim shouted so loudly that Nancy turned around and stared at her in surprise. Then she noticed Carrie.

"Wow!" she said. "Wow! Carrie, you look sensational. You're so pretty, I can't believe it."

Carrie's face got warm. "You mean I was that bad?"

"No, course not. It's just that . . . that . . ." Nancy floundered.

"It's just that you didn't notice me."

Nancy looked embarrassed and didn't know what to say.

"That's a thing of the past," Kim piped up. "And it all has to do with antennae."

"Antennae?" Nancy was puzzled.

"That's exactly what I mean!"

"You mean those things on the heads of insects that send and receive waves?"

"That's right," Carrie assured her.

"I think I'm beginning to understand. When it comes to giving out messages, there's nobody like Sam." She turned once again to gaze at Sam's picture.

"You're hopeless," Kim teased, and Carrie nodded her head in agreement. Then the two girls exchanged a delighted and knowing smile.

Chapter 4

*K*im and Carrie had just come from computer science, the last class of the day, and their heads were spinning. The teacher, Mr. Kushel, who was regarded as a young Einstein, tossed out terms that he assumed everyone was familiar with. He wasn't too wrong, because most of the kids had taken a course in computer science at their previous schools, or learned how to operate a word processor at their mother's knee. Kim and Carrie decided they were the exceptions, and they were determined to catch up.

"The first thing we've got to do is learn the language," Carrie said as they ambled toward their dorm.

"Right. There's a glossary at the back of our textbook, and if we can figure out what all those abbreviations stand for, we'll be on our way. Kushel talks about bits and pips as though they were ABCs."

"Why don't we bone up on this separately right now? Ginger and Nancy are never around at this hour. I'll come to your room in about forty minutes and we'll test each other," Carrie suggested.

"Terrific idea. After all, we're not used to being at the bottom of the class."

"We won't be for long," Carrie said. "Our reputations are at stake."

Then they both nodded their heads, knowing that what Carrie said was true. They had to maintain good grades in all their courses if they were to continue receiving a scholarship. With that thought in mind, they marched with more determination than ever to their rooms.

Kim sat at her desk chewing the end of a pencil and muttering to herself: "CCP—console command processor, the section of CP/M that makes sense of what you type on the keyboard. CRT—cathode ray tube, the tube that's used as the video display on the computer."

She was only up to the Cs when there was a rap on the door.

"Come in," she said eagerly, expecting to see Carrie, who she thought was probably finding this memorizing just as tedious as she was and decided to come early.

"Hi, hope this isn't a bad time." Renée Maxwell, one of the most important seniors on campus, swept into the room and closed the door behind her. Renée lived in the next house, was famous for her acting ability, and was considered one of the best writers on the literary magazine. In addition she looked as though she might have posed for the cover of *Seventeen*.

"No, it's a good time," Kim assured her, and tried not to show her surprise. "I'm trying to master the meaning of bits and boots, and I'm not talking about horseback riding!"

Renée laughed. "Mind if I sit down?"

"Please do," Kim said, and pointed to the easy chair, which was occupied by her tattered teddy bear. "Just push Bolívar over. He doesn't mind."

Renée carefully placed Bolívar on the bed, and then sat down.

"You're probably wondering why I'm bere," she began.

"Kind of," Kim answered, trying not to show she was bursting with curiosity.

"Before I tell you, will you promise to keep this conversation private, no matter what you decide?"

"I'm not sure," Kim said slowly. "Until you tell me, I can't promise anything."

"That's a very good answer, and that's one of the reasons we thought you'd be perfect."

"Perfect? Perfect for what?"

"Let me begin by saying we love Adams, it's a terrific school and all that, but it is rigid. Don't you agree?"

"There are a zillion rules," Kim said. "Lights Out at ten, required study period after supper, no jeans, having to sign in at breakfast—and I love to sleep in—no boys allowed except in the lounge at certain hours, and on and on."

"Exactly!" Renée said triumphantly. "It's even worse when you're a senior like me, and you've been told what you can't wear and what time to go to bed for three years."

"I guess I'll feel that way, too, but there's not much we can do about it."

"Not openly, we can't."

"What do you mean?"

Renée leaned forward conspiratorially and lowered her voice. "There's a secret club on campus called the Sine Nomine, which means 'No name.' I'm one of the officers and founding members."

"Really!" Kim's eyes widened.

"It all began when I was a freshman and we wanted to stretch our muscles, feel we had a little more control over our lives. Nothing really bad . . . just breaking a few rules."

"Like what?" Kim was fascinated.

"Like secret meetings after Lights Out; smoking, which is absolutely forbidden; switching rooms some nights; having code names for teachers; helping one of us meet her boyfriend after curfew. We have a special handshake and our own song that binds us together forever." Renée ran out of breath. "Now you know everything about us, except the final initiation rite. That's kept secret from the initiates."

"Sounds exciting." Kim's eyes sparkled.

"Believe me, it is. And the truth is, the best kids in the school belong."

"How many?"

"Sixteen. That's the most we ever want. Four of us are graduating and we want to make sure S.N.—that's how we refer to The Club—continues. So we're recruiting replacements."

"That shouldn't be difficult."

"It's not, but we don't take just anyone. We're highly selective. You see, it's a privilege to belong."

"I guess so," Kim remarked thoughtfully. "Can you tell me who else you're considering?"

"So far we've only absolutely agreed on you and Pam Hopkins. She's that terrific-looking long-haired blonde who lives in Franklin. She's a diplomat's daughter and speaks three foreign languages fluently."

"Sure I know her. I played her in the tryouts for the junior varsity basketball team and she was sensational. We both made the team, but she's going to be a star."

"That's the kind of girl we're looking for."

Kim nodded her head, then asked point-blank, "Are you considering Carrie Gordon?"

Renée frowned slightly. "She's that tall thin girl who lives in Ellsworth?"

"That's right."

31

"To tell the truth, we never gave her too much thought. She seems so quiet and . . ."

Renée suddenly stopped talking, realizing that Kim had mentioned her for a reason. It dawned on her that she'd seen Kim and Carrie hanging out together more than once, and that maybe they were best friends. Getting Kim to join The Club might well depend on whether Carrie was also invited.

"None of us know Carrie too well, but if you think she'd be a good candidate . . . " Renée continued.

"I think she'd be great." Kim was so adamant that Renée was sure that no Carrie meant no Kim.

"We haven't made any firm decisions yet, and it certainly won't hurt to talk to her. We're still at the 'chatting up' stage, which means what we're doing now."

"It works both ways, doesn't it?" Kim asked. "I mean after talking to someone, you may decide against her."

"That's happened a few times, and then we let her know as tactfully as possible that she wouldn't enjoy being a member."

"Or maybe you've wanted someone to join, but she wasn't interested."

"That happened only once. We never did find out why."

"Well, I am interested, but I don't want to give a fast answer. I think you should talk to Carrie. I know she's in her room—Room 301 at the end of the hall—and you could chat her up right now."

"Okay, I'll do that," Renée said, standing up. "The one risk we take in these first rounds is that someone we're considering might talk about The Club, and then we're finished. So far, that's never happened."

"I can see why that might be a problem, but I promise you can count on Carrie and me. I think whoever squealed would be the worst kind of fink!"

Renée smiled. "You are the kind of member we want, Kim, and I do hope you'll join."

"I'll certainly think about it. When do you want to know?"

"Day after tomorrow. I'll come by same time, if it's okay."

"See you then," Kim said, "and I'll have my answer."

Renée left the room, more convinced than ever that Kim's joining depended on Carrie. That might be the bad news. On the other hand, the good news was that Kim was so outstanding she'd never be tight with someone who wasn't also special.

Kim went back to studying the computer vocabulary, but she read the definition of DIR—"A built-in CP/M command that lists names of all files on a diskette"—three times before she realized that her brain wasn't registering. She was too excited about Renée's visit and hearing about The Club to concentrate.

Kim had tried to act cool in Renée's presence, but her heart was pounding. She could hardly wait until Carrie came in and they could talk about it. There was no doubt in her mind that she wanted to join, and that Carrie would, too. The idea of being picked for a secret club was thrilling.

She decided it was useless to try to do any homework, so she changed into her purple leotard, put on a Neil Young tape, and started to do some exercises. That was mindless and would make the time pass until Carrie arrived.

Kim had completed a series of stretches and was standing on her head when Carrie appeared at the door.

"Come in, come in," Kim squeaked in an upside-down position.

"Is that a new way of studying?" Carrie teased. She walked toward the bed, picked up Bolívar, and sat down.

Kim lowered her legs and, still on her knees, stared at Carrie, trying to gauge her reaction. "Who can study after what we just heard?"

"You mean about The Club?"

"Sshhh," Kim cautioned, then quickly crawled to the door and slammed it shut. "Aren't you amazed?"

"I am rather surprised, but I don't think it's such a big deal."

"You don't?" Kim fell back on the floor, crestfallen.

"I don't know if I want to join, even if I'm asked."

"Are you serious?"

"Dead serious. I guess you feel just the opposite."

"I sure do, and you should, too."

"Renée does make it sound like the greatest thing since sliced bread, but I don't know. . . ."

Kim jumped up, placed her hands on her hips, and asked with as much patience as she could muster, "What exactly don't you know?"

"Whether I want to join," Carrie said mildly.

"But why wouldn't you?"

"I don't know." Carrie looked absently at Bolívar.

"Bolívar doesn't know the answer, but I can give you a few why you should."

"Go ahead."

Kim took a deep breath and flopped down in the easy chair. Her initial disappointment in her friend diminished as she reminded herself that Carrie's upbringing had been a lot different from hers, and that as a result Carrie was much less adventuresome.

"Look, Carrie," Kim said gently, "you have to take a few risks in life. You already told me that you never knew what it was like to have a gang of friends. This is your opportunity to change all that."

"Maybe. Why do you think so?"

"I get the impression that S.N. members really stick together, and they wouldn't be asking us if they didn't think we would fit right in."

"They haven't asked us officially. Renée said she'd be back in two days to talk some more. Is that what she said to you?"

Kim thought fast. She didn't want to lie, but she knew Carrie suspected the real reason she'd been interviewed. Kim certainly wasn't going to let on that if she agreed to join, Carrie would be a shoo-in.

"Renée told me she'd be here the day after tomorrow, same time, same place," she answered honestly. Then she quickly added, "I think it'll be so much fun. I can't see any reason not to join."

"What if we're discovered? It might be we'd be put on probation, or worse yet, expelled."

"The chances of that are one in a zillion. They've been operating for three years and nothing's happened. Besides, the worst thing anyone's done, from what Renée tells me, is sneak out after curfew."

"What happens if someone's caught?"

"Probably the worst thing is she'd be confined to her dorm for a weekend, or put on penalty crew. That's not the end of the world."

"Penalty crew can be a real bummer," Carrie argued. "You know that means getting up Sunday at eight o'clock and raking leaves for four hours, or shoveling snow, or cleaning stables, or worse yet, getting kitchen duty."

"I know, but half the fun is trying to get away with something. And we're all in it together. If we are found out, they're not going to kick out sixteen of the best kids in the school!"

"I guess you're right about that. I am inclined to be on the cautious side," Carrie admitted.

"You sure are," Kim said with affection. "Look, you've already changed your image by wearing a little makeup . . . thanks to me."

Carrie grinned. "Even Renée noticed. She said, 'There's something different about you from the way I first remember you. You're much more vivid.' I tried not to laugh."

"See, listen to me!" Kim was gleeful.

"Maybe I should."

"There's no question. Belonging to a secret club is just what we need. School shouldn't be all work, you know."

"I know."

"Then if we're asked, you'll join?"

Carrie hesitated. "You're going to, aren't you?"

"Not if you don't, Carrie. It won't be nearly as much fun if we're not in it together."

Carrie was flattered and pleased. "How can I say no when you put it like that?"

"You can't," Kim said matter-of-factly.

"Then I'll say yes. As you say, I have to learn to take risks."

Chapter 5

*K*im couldn't wait to get through the next two days. She had tried not to think about The Club, but it was always in the back of her mind. She hoped there wouldn't be a slip-up—that Carrie wouldn't panic at the last minute about breaking the rules and refuse to join, that the leaders wouldn't change their minds about wanting them for members.

Now the Day of Decision had arrived, and Kim, who had given up biting her nails in kindergarten, found herself staring out the window, nervously chewing on her little fingernail and impatiently waiting for Renée. She'd only been in her room eight minutes, which seemed more like hours, when she heard footsteps approaching. She'd left her door ajar and tried to appear casual when Renée, who had stuck her head in, asked, "Can we come in?"

"We? Who's we? I mean, sure, come in," Kim said, and whipped around. Her jaw dropped when she saw Ellen, who was following right behind Renée, carefully closing the door.

"You're a member?" Kim breathed.

Ellen chuckled. "I guess I have the reputation for being the perfect Adams student—president of Ellsworth and on the student council and captain of the swimming team and all that—but what makes everything possible is S.N."

"Really?" Kim exclaimed, not quite recovered from the shock. Ellen, since she was a highly visible figure on campus, was the last person in the world Kim could imagine even bending a rule, much less breaking one.

"It's the greatest," Ellen said. "I hope you've decided to join us."

Before Kim could say anything, Renée wanted her to know that Carrie had been approved for membership also. She quickly piped up, "We're going to see Carrie next, and I thank you for bringing her to our attention. Our spies tell us that she's a brilliant student, and very diversified in her interests. In the orchestra and the science club as well."

Kim was pleased with herself, thinking she'd done both Carrie and The Club a favor.

"I hope you've decided to join us," Ellen repeated.

"I have," Kim answered enthusiastically, "I have."

"That's wonderful," Renée said. "As of now, you are a junior member. That allows you to take part in all our meetings and to learn all our secrets. Once you have gone through the final initiation rite, you will be designated a senior member and receive a pin specially designed for S.N."

"Can't wait," Kim said. "When and where do we meet?"

"One thing you should know," Ellen told her, "is that we don't have a regular meeting place or time. It's one of the reasons we haven't been discovered."

"I thought we always met after Lights Out."

"Only sometimes. That's too dangerous to do every

week. This week, for example, we're going to meet Tuesday at five-thirty in the garden shed at the west end of the lake. No one hangs out there this time of year, and though it'll be a little crowded, it's safe."

"What a good idea!" Kim was more and more enthralled.

"We better get going now," Renée said. "But one last thing before we go, you must learn our handshake and motto."

Kim observed carefully as Renée and Ellen grasped each other's wrist, shook their arms up and down three times, then briefly locked their thumbs together and intoned, "S.N. now and forever." They repeated the same maneuver and words with Kim.

Kim beamed as she watched them leave, and unconsciously crossed her fingers and hoped as hard as she could that everything would go as smoothly for Carrie. In order to kill time, she decided to straighten out her bureau drawers, but every few minutes she peered down the hall to see if Renée and Ellen had completed their mission. After fifteen minutes, she saw them come out of Carrie's door and disappear down the stairs. Then Kim raced down the hall and barged into Carrie's room. Carrie was just about to head for Kim's room, so the two of them collided, and Carrie was knocked backward.

"Sorry," Kim gasped, helping Carrie to gain her balance. "I can hardly wait to hear what happened. How did it go?"

"Perfect," Carrie answered, straightening herself up. Now that she was no longer on trial, and had been officially made a junior member of Sine Nomine, her defenses had promptly evaporated. To show how delighted she was, she extended her arm, grasped Kim's wrist, shook it up and down three times, locked thumbs, and affirmed with as much dignity as possible, "S.N. now and forever."

"S.N. now and forever," Kim repeated in an equally somber voice. Then, unable to maintain their serious demeanor, they both collapsed into a fit of laughter.

"Adams is going to be more fun than I ever imagined," Carrie said.

"You know it!" Kim agreed.

"Why don't we go into town and celebrate with an ice cream soda at the Frost Bite? It'll fortify us for supper, which I heard is going to be camel ears on a bed of rice."

"Good idea. And there's still time to buy a poster. Your side of the room needs something." Kim frowned at the bare wall over Carrie's bed.

"I'm beginning to think you're right. I thought maybe a portrait of Mozart or Bach."

"I was thinking more along the idea of the Solarflex man."

"You would," Carrie said, grinning, and took her wallet out of her desk drawer. "I'll sign us out while you get your things."

"Okay, see you downstairs." Kim took another despairing look at Carrie's blank wall. "Not Mozart or Bach," she pleaded.

"Well, maybe John Lennon."

"That's the spirit!" Kim said, and skipped out.

Ginger, under a mound of bedclothes, opened one eye and peered at her roommate, who was already dressed in a pale-gray skirt and white shirt. "Sunday's supposed to be a day of rest," she mumbled.

"I know, but Mr. Crowley called a special rehearsal because he wants to work on 'The Swan' by Saint-Saëns."

"On Sunday?"

"He sweetened the invitation by offering us high tea after the rehearsal. He's English, you know. Looks like a stern banker, but I know has the soul of an artist."

"You must really love music—or tea."

"Both."

"And it doesn't hurt that there are boys there."

"To tell the truth, I haven't really noticed."

"If I didn't know you so well, I wouldn't believe you. Have fun anyway."

Ginger sighed, rolled over, and buried her head in her pillow.

Just as Carrie was leaving with her flute case, she noticed Kim coming out of the bathroom at the end of the hall. Kim was still in her pajamas and motioned Carrie toward her.

"This is Sunday," Kim remarked, appraising Carrie from head to toe as she approached. "No classes, and we're allowed to wear jeans. Have you forgotten what day it is?"

"Ginger thought I was crazy, too," Carrie said, and then explained why she was up so early.

"You're going to rehearsal, and you look very nice, but do me a favor and wear my red sweater. It'll go great with what you have on."

"Your favorite sweater?"

"Why not? I'm going to try horseback riding with some guys I met in theater class. I'm willing to risk breaking my neck, but I sure don't want to take a chance on ruining my sweater. It's just lying in the drawer. Come get it, but don't make any noise. Nancy's still zzzzzing."

The two girls slipped quietly into the room. Kim promptly brought out the sweater and tied the arms around Carrie's shoulders. "You may not need it for warmth, but it's pure glamour," she whispered.

Carrie glanced at herself in the mirror and nodded her

head vigorously. "Thanks," she breathed, "I'll take very good care of it. Now I've got to run before I'm late."

She raced down the stairs and started across the campus, when a couple of other girls toting violin cases bounded out of the next house and saw her.

"Wait up, Carrie," one of them shouted. "Let's all arrive together. If we're even two minutes late, I hear Crowley might have a tantrum."

"I've heard that too," Carrie said, slowing her pace until they caught up.

It was a sparkling sunny day, and it perfectly suited Carrie's mood. She had no logical explanation, but as she jogged around the lake with the two other musicians, and they beefed about Crowley and his stuffy English ways, she felt more as if she were going to a party than to a rehearsal.

The girls slid into their seats as the clock struck nine—not a moment to spare—and immediately started warming up. Several other orchestra members straggled in over the next ten minutes while Mr. Crowley paced up and down in front of the podium.

Carrie was grateful that she wasn't the recipient of the glowering stare he radared at them. She had carefully placed the sweater on the back of her chair, and now she patted it as though it were responsible for bringing her luck.

Mr. Crowley, finally satisfied that all the orchestra had arrived, climbed to the podium and briskly rapped the music stand with his baton. There was immediate silence.

"I wish you people who are late would realize how much you punish the people who are on time." He waited a full minute while the latecomers twitched, turned red, or slouched down in their seats.

Then he pointed to the oboist. "Let's have an A," he said, and for the next twenty seconds there was the squawky sound of the orchestra tuning up.

"Okay," Mr. Crowley said, his hands poised for a downbeat, "Let's take 'The Swan' from the top."

From the very first bars, Carrie was aware she was listening to a talented cellist. He seemed to be one with his instrument, and Carrie wondered who he was. She was in the back of the string section but had a clear view of his profile. He seemed quite tall, even sitting down. His sandy-colored hair curled a little at the nape of his neck, and his narrow nose gave him a slightly aesthetic look. He wore a navy blue T-shirt and khakis, and Carrie thought, Talented *and* cute.

Carrie felt her heart beat faster, although that was often the case when she got involved in music. Still, she found herself looking at the soloist more than was usual, and when she almost missed an entrance, she made a super effort to focus on the conductor.

When the piece was finished, the orchestra members shuffled their feet, an orchestra's way of showing their appreciation of the soloist's performance. Mr. Crowley raised his hands for silence and tilted his head in the cellist's direction.

"Our soloist is fine, but let's get down to what really needs work—the orchestral accompaniment."

For the rest of the session he drilled the notes of "The Swan" until he was satisfied that every player had them down solid, and then he worked on a couple of movements of the "Military" symphony of Haydn. Carrie was still peculiarly distracted but managed to get through the rehearsal without any fluffs.

When it was over, Mr. Crowley thanked the orchestra for coming. "We've got a lot done, but as you can hear, we still have a long way to go. I'll see you at our regular rehearsal time next week. Are there any questions?"

"What about tea?" Max, the flamboyant percussionist, asked.

"Of course, it is teatime. Next door in the large practice room." Mr. Crowley spoke in such an understated manner that the most anyone hoped for was boiling water and a box of tea bags.

Since no one had had time for breakfast, there was a mad scramble as the entire orchestra packed up their instruments and left the rehearsal hall. Carrie tossed the red sweater around her shoulders, and crowded with the others into the practice room. She, along with everyone else, was astounded to see two long tables laden with a variety of biscuits, crumpets, croissants, jams, and marmalade. Several samovars were heating up, and Carrie waited patiently while the most eager helped themselves.

Suddenly, someone bumped into her from behind, so that the sweater half slid off her back.

"Uh-oh," an apologetic male voice said, and Carrie felt two strong hands firmly place the sweater on her shoulders.

Carrie turned to see who was behind her, and found herself face to face with the soloist. "It's you!" she exclaimed, staring into his deep brown eyes. She felt her heart thumping again.

"I'm sorry," he muttered, looking embarrassed.

"That's okay. I mean you didn't do it on purpose."

"No. Of course not. All these tea hounds . . ."

Carrie waited for him to say something else, but he just stood there and smiled shyly.

For the first time in her life, Carrie knew it was up to her to keep the conversation rolling. "That was really beautiful cello playing."

"Thank you," he said.

"A lot of people don't realize that playing slow sustained notes is more difficult than playing fast."

"You're right," he said, looking at her appreciatively. "I suppose that's also true of the flute."

"Is it ever!" she said, delighted that she got him to respond and also that he must have noticed what instrument she played.

"My teacher actually had me blow a single note for a full minute. I thought I might faint."

"I do pretty much the same thing with my bowing arm."

"I think the slowest piece I ever played was by Gluck."

"You mean the lament from *Orfeo*?"

"Yes, that's exactly what I mean. That's really tough."

"I can believe it."

The two of them stood there for the longest time, talking about music, while the crowd dwindled. They were so absorbed in each other that they forgot where they were, until someone brushed by and said, "Carrie, you better fuel up before it's all gone."

"Huh," Carrie said, and saw that it was one of the violinists she had walked with to the rehearsal.

"Food"—she pointed to her mouth—"it's practically all gone."

"Oh yeah, thanks." Carrie was only interested in resuming her conversation with the cellist, and turned back to him.

"Your name's Carrie," he said.

"Carrie Gordon. What's yours?"

"Mark Newman. This must be your first year, or I would have noticed you."

As soon as he spoke those words, he looked very uncomfortable. Carrie sensed that he wasn't used to talking to girls and the compliment had just slipped out.

"It is my first year," she said quickly, "and I'm a sophomore. What about you?"

"I'm a junior. This is my second year. Tell me, why did you . . ."

"Hey, Mark," the percussionist called loudly from the far corner of the room, where he was sitting with a couple of girls on a piano bench, "are you two planning a duet or something? This is supposed to be breakfast time."

There was a ripple of laughter and Carrie didn't know whether to laugh or cry at the situation, but she was miraculously rescued by Mark, who said evenly, "Thanks for reminding us, Max."

Carrie was so pleased and curiously proud of Mark that she was able to manage a smile and say, "I think they're trying to tell us something."

"I think you're right," Mark said, grinning back at her. Then he impulsively pulled her by the arm toward the tea table.

"Talking to you, I forgot all about breakfast," Carrie admitted, and filled a plate with some biscuits and jam.

"Certain things can do that to you," Mark said.

He had turned on the samovar and was holding a cup under it. Not until the tea spilled over the brim and splashed onto his hand did he realize he hadn't been paying attention to anything but Carrie. "Ouch!" he cried, and quickly turned off the faucet.

Carrie grabbed a bunch of paper napkins and gently blotted his hand. "Are you okay?" she asked.

"I'm wonderful," he said. "I mean my hand's wonderful." He looked at Carrie again with that shy smile that made her want to hug him.

When they finally managed to get the tea poured, Mark weaved his way to the side of the room, where there were a couple of empty chairs.

"This requires more coordination than playing the cello," Mark remarked as he sat down, holding a biscuit in one hand and a teacup in the other.

Carrie giggled. "I don't think I can stand making any more scenes for Max."

"Forget about Max. Before he interrupted I was about to ask you why you happened to come to Adams."

Carrie proceeded to tell him, and then confided that her dream was to study medicine and play in the physicians' orchestra. She was still going on when Mr. Crowley announced that teatime was over.

"If we don't break now, we'll be late for lunch. But please, before you go, unload your plates and cups in the receptacles that were designed for that purpose."

Carrie was astounded when she realized how much time she had spent talking about herself to a boy, and a complete stranger. But he didn't seem like a stranger, and he was so interested.

"I guess we have to leave," she said wistfully.

"I guess so."

There was an awkward silence, and then they both started to speak at the same time. Neither of them could be understood, and they burst out laughing.

"What were you about to say?" Carrie asked.

Mark took a deep breath, as though he were about to plunge into dangerous waters. "I hope I see you again, Carrie, and I don't mean just at the rehearsal."

"I hope so, too," Carrie murmured.

Then they gazed deeply into each other's eyes, expressing more with their silent looks than they ever could with words. There was a lot of bustling around them, but they didn't notice until Max, in his usual brash manner, passed by them with a pile of paper plates and cups.

"Hey you two, it's clean-up time. The party's over."

This time neither Carrie nor Mark was the least bit rattled. And when Max was clearly out of earshot, Mark said softly, "What he doesn't know is that it's just beginning."

47

Chapter 6

*M*ark and Carrie were the last ones to leave the music building. Mark lugged his cello case outside, with Carrie by his side, and then deliberately stopped and placed it on the ground. He turned to look at her.

"Well," he said, "I promised myself I'd spend the afternoon cramming for a physics exam I have tomorrow morning. I've spent so much time preparing for my solo that I temporarily gave up doing any homework. What are you going to do?"

Carrie shrugged her shoulders. "Don't know. It's such a beautiful day, I don't want to spend it inside."

Mark frowned thoughtfully. "Me neither. The truth is, a few hours of studying the interaction of matter and energy is enough."

"Then you'll need a break."

Mark's face lit up. "Exactly! How about meeting me this afternoon at the boys' pier and I'll take you on a private tour of our campus?"

"I'd like that. I've never really seen the boys' campus."

Carrie tried not to show how ridiculously pleased she was with the invitation.

"Three o'clock okay?"

"I'll be there."

Carrie returned to the girls' school and climbed the stairs to her room in a daze. She was relieved to find that Ellsworth was deserted and she didn't have to exchange hi's with anyone or answer questions about the rehearsal. It was lunchtime, and all the girls were either in the dining hall or doing their own thing. Sunday was the one free day at Adams, nothing was required, and Carrie wallowed in the freedom.

For the next ten minutes, she made a feeble attempt to do some studying. After all, that's what Mark was doing. But nothing grabbed her. Reading about the Crusades was almost as boring as conjugating French verbs. The only thing she could think about was getting ready for her "date."

It had never been a particular concern, but now she worried about what to wear. Jeans, she decided, was the most appropriate garb, but what top? She dragged every shirt out of her closet, held them up to her, and viewed her image in the mirror. Everything was woefully dull, except for a pale pink long-sleeved cotton—sporty but feminine. It enhanced her natural coloring, especially if she helped it along with some of the cosmetic tricks Kim had taught her.

She flipped on the radio, switched from her usual classical program to a pop station, and spent longer than she ever had in her life putting on her face and fixing her hair. After appraising herself in the mirror, and being satisfied with the result, she danced blissfully around the room to a jazzed-up version of "Fly Me to the Moon." That's exactly the sentiment she was feeling, and when Ginger unexpectedly rushed into the room she was singing out loud.

"Forgot this," Ginger shouted above the music as she grabbed her riding crop from her corner. She was about to hurry out when she noticed Carrie, who had abruptly stopped gyrating to the music and had struck what she hoped was a relaxed pose against the table that divided the room. But she was still breathless, and Ginger knew something was up.

"What's come over you?" she asked in her outspoken way.

"What do you mean?" Carrie hoped she sounded innocent, but she wasn't good at dissembling. And there was no way she could hide the quirky smile on her lips.

Ginger leaned against her desk and looked at her indulgently, as though Carrie were a three-year-old caught with her hand in the cookie jar. "For starters, I could hear that music blasting away before I even set foot in the building. This was the last place I thought it'd be coming from."

"I was just in the mood for something different."

"Sure," Ginger said, "one heavy rehearsal and you're driven toward rock."

"Guess so." Carrie knew she sounded silly.

"The other thing, you've done a terrific job on your eyes. Even half-asleep I could see you weren't wearing eye shadow this morning."

"Didn't have time."

"Course not." Ginger spoke with just a touch of sarcasm.

"It's true," Carrie said, defending herself. "I did have to get out of here on time."

"I have another theory, Carrie."

"Like what?" Carrie couldn't resist asking.

"Like with you waltzing around with a glazed look to *my* music, and that midday makeup job, and that pretty pink

50

shirt—which I've never seen you in before—I think you've got the symptoms of a peculiar malaise that I've had a few times myself."

"A peculiar malaise? You mean a funny sickness?"

"Something like that."

"Come on, Ginger. What are you saying?"

"I'm saying, Carrie, that you've got all the signs of falling in love."

Carrie blushed, but she couldn't deny that Ginger was right on target.

"I always knew you were smart," Carrie told her.

"Didn't take much," Ginger said. "Now I must go. My Sir Galahad awaits me."

"Your Sir Galahad? Who's he?" Carrie looked puzzled.

"My Sir Galahad has four legs, a long tail, and a beautiful black coat that he never changes."

"Oh, your horse!" Carrie exclaimed.

"I'm happy your brains aren't completely scrambled," Ginger teased and dashed out of the room. Carrie could hear her chuckling all the way down the stairs.

"*My* Sir Galahad awaits me," Carrie murmured to herself as she once again put the red sweater around her shoulders. Then, in answer to the imagined question "Who's he?" she replied dreamily, "He's tall and sensitive and has this adorable smile and his name is Mark."

Since she wasn't expected for twenty minutes, Carrie took her time wending her way to the boys' pier. It didn't occur to her to arrive late in order not to appear anxious. As she sauntered around the lake, she wondered what the point was in playing games with boys as a lot of girls did—being hard to get, pretending that you didn't like someone when you really did, paying attention to another boy in order to make the one you did like jealous. It went against her logical mind.

She was so deep in these thoughts that she was less than thirty feet from the pier when she realized Mark was already there. He was sitting on the back of a bench that ran along the dock and he must have been watching her circle the lake.

Carrie was flustered until he jumped down, all smiles, and said, "A little of the quantum theory goes a long way. I decided to get here early and commune with nature."

"I didn't feel like studying either."

"I guess we better get started. I know you have to check in at five-thirty or you'll be in trouble. I'd hate to be responsible for you getting on penalty crew."

"Don't worry about that," Carrie said, surprising herself at her devil-may-care attitude. "But I would like to see your campus. Where do we begin?"

"I thought we'd take it from the top, starting with the dorms, the administration hall, and the study centers. Then I'll show you the athletic fields and the orchards."

As they strolled along, Mark and Carrie told each other about their families, interspersed with Mark pointing out the various buildings. They discovered they had similar reasons for coming to Adams. Mark's high school, in a small suburb in North Carolina where his father was a doctor, didn't have the challenges that Adams provided.

"The music program was practically nonexistent, and since that's my thing, my parents encouraged me to come here."

"Are you glad you made the switch?"

"I like it better every day." He glanced at Carrie sideways and she hoped that remark had something to do with her.

He told Carrie that he got along great with his parents, except when it came to sports.

"They're worried about your hands," Carrie stated.

"That's right! We had this big hassle about me playing any contact sports, and I finally saw their point of view. If I want to be a musician, I have to protect my hands. A broken finger could set me back for months, and I decided it wasn't worth it."

"So you compromised, and went out for track."

Mark looked at her in amazement. "You're a mind reader! How'd you know?"

"It just figures. You've got long legs and . . . and rhythm."

"That's all it takes, I guess, because I'm on the varsity track team." Mark looked very pleased with himself.

"I bet you're a good dancer, too." Carrie, who had always been reserved around boys, was alarmed at her personal remark. She bit her lip before she made a complete fool of herself, and was relieved that Mark went right on talking.

"You'll find out at the mixer next Saturday. You're going, aren't you?"

"Probably." Carrie hadn't given the mixer much thought, although a lot of the girls were talking about it. "Are they fun?"

"They will be now," Mark said softly, and this time Carrie was sure that what he said had everything to do with her.

Carrie wanted that afternoon to go on forever, but before she knew it, the chapel bell had sounded five o'clock. They were sitting under an apple tree in the orchard, their backs leaning against the tree trunk, their shoulders barely touching. They both knew the rules—no physical contact between the sexes allowed on campus. Since teachers, as well as students, intermittently passed by, Mark and Carrie didn't even hold hands.

"Time to go," Mark said gloomily. He stood up, reached for Carrie's hand, and pulled her to her feet.

"This was a wonderful tour," Carrie said as they ambled toward the pier.

"I think you've seen everything but the boathouse. We'll take that in right now."

The boathouse was a narrow clapboard structure next to the dock. Mark led the way in, and they stood still, blinking in order to accustom themselves to the darkness. There were two small windows facing the lake, which allowed enough light for Carrie to see the shapes of several canoes and rowboats, oars and paddles on racks, and life preservers hung on the walls.

Carrie moved toward the window. "The lake is beautiful now," she said.

Mark stood next to her and didn't say anything. Carrie sensed that his shyness had returned, and she was suddenly at a loss for words herself.

Then Mark turned to face her, put his arms on her shoulders, and drew her close. He slowly bent his head down and pressed his lips against hers, gently at first, and then more and more firmly. When they drew apart, he whispered, "Carrie . . . I . . . ."

"What?" Carrie asked breathlessly.

"This was the best day I've ever had."

"Me too," Carrie said.

Once again, Mark pulled her to him and covered her mouth with his lips. Carrie knew then what it meant to melt in someone's arms.

* * *

Carrie wasn't sure how, but she got back to her dorm and floated up the stairs. The first thing she did was head for Kim's room. Nancy was just leaving, and mumbled something about needing to get change for her call to Sam.

"Come in," Kim said. "I was looking for you. Where've you been?"

"To the moon," Carrie sighed mistily.

"You better sit down," Kim said, pointing to her bed. "You look a little weak."

"Something like that," Carrie said. She collapsed on the bed, but not before she removed the red sweater and hugged it to her.

"That must have been some rehearsal." Kim sat on the edge of the bed, gently took the sweater from Carrie, and looked at her quizzically.

"The rehearsal was a hundred years ago."

"It was only this morning. Then what happened?"

"There's this boy, Mark, and he took me on a tour."

"And that's how you got to the moon?"

"After we went to the boathouse."

"And then?"

"And then . . . what Ginger calls my peculiar malaise got worse, or better. Depending on how you look at it."

"You're not being your usual rational self."

"That's one of the symptoms."

"In other words, you're in love!" Kim exclaimed.

Carrie didn't have to say anything. Her mile-wide grin told it all.

Kim hopped up from the bed and gleefully spun around in a circle holding the sweater in front of her. "I told you this had magical powers."

"You sure did." Carrie sighed happily. "There's no other way I could have been flown to the moon."

Chapter 7

*W*ord was passed along that although the S.N. meeting would begin promptly at five-thirty, the members should arrive separately two minutes apart. That way, attention would not be drawn to them. Carrie was told to be there at five-twenty-seven, and she was precisely on time. By five-thirty everyone was crowded into the shed, which was half-filled with rakes, hoes, shovels, and other outdoor equipment. The girls sat on the built-in benches and folding chairs, or leaned against the wall.

Renée, who was half sitting on a workbench, welcomed everyone, introduced the new girls, and said, "We might as well start the school year right by having a weed."

She dug into her canvas bag, took out a book of matches and a new pack of long-stemmed cigarettes, deftly ripped it open, withdrew one, lighted up, and passed the pack and matches to the person next to her.

Carrie knew that smoking was an infraction of the rules, but something about doing it so furtively made it seem absolutely sinful. That idea, plus the fact that she had never tried a cigarette before, made her stomach knot up. She would have liked to refuse, but how could she do so gracefully? She glanced at Kim, who was standing against the wall, and hoped to get a clue from her about what to do.

Carrie had her answer in seconds, for Kim had just accepted a cigarette. Then she expertly ignited it, and took a deep drag. Carrie felt the knot in her stomach tighten as each girl unhesitatingly did the same. She would have to fake it, or be branded a superwimp.

By the time it was Carrie's turn, the air was blue with smoke. She thought this might be an advantage—if she was lucky, no one would see her fumbling through the misty haze. But this was wishful thinking. Maybe because she was on trial, or more likely because it took her three matches before she could even get started, fifteen pairs of eyes were suddenly focused on her.

She inhaled deeply, as everyone else had done, but instead of blowing the smoke out, she assumed it would float away by simply opening her mouth. Before she could figure out what went wrong, she began to cough so violently that her face turned red and tears spilled down her cheeks.

Jennifer Corry, the fourth junior member, who was an energetic blonde and had already earned a reputation at Adams as a star photographer, was sitting next to Carrie and pounded her on the back. Carrie's head was spinning, and she thought she might throw up or pass out. She hoped for the latter, because then she wouldn't have to face these girls, all of whom seemed so sophisticated.

But the coughing subsided, and Carrie steeled herself against what she expected to be a bombardment of ridicule. Instead, she heard Renée saying, "This happens to all of us in the beginning. Nothing to worry about, Carrie."

The others took their cue from Renée, and everything they said was reassuring. "First time I smoked, I burned my hand." "That's nothing. I dropped the cigarette and burned the rug. I thought my father would kill me." "I barfed." There were so many descriptions of disaster that Carrie wondered why anyone would smoke in the first place and how they could ever get addicted.

"Ready to try once more?" Ellen asked.

"You should," someone said. "It's like falling off a horse. Get right back on or you may never ride again."

"Sure I'm ready," Carrie said.

There was lots of advice offered: "Don't inhale at first." "Take small puffs." "Blow the smoke out." "Go slow." "Don't breathe deeply."

"This is really an art," Carrie joked. Then, although her hand was shaking, she successfully lit up on the first try and took a puff, then another, and another. When she stopped, there was a round of applause and exclamations of approval. Carrie thought of herself as a heroine, and she knew it wasn't because she'd mastered such a stupid accomplishment as smoking. It was because for the first time in her life she felt she belonged.

This feeling was reinforced when the next order of business was for the members to familiarize themselves with the code names of the teachers and update the list. Suggestions were offered for new members of the faculty, including Mr. Crowley. After much discussion and no agreement, Carrie tentatively came up with "The Penguin," which was unanimously accepted as being absolutely perfect for this rather stuffy Englishman. Carrie was ridiculously pleased with her suggestion being approved.

Then Renée asked if there were any problems S.N. might solve. Hilary, one of the senior members, raised her hand.

"I've got a major problem," she began. "My boyfriend from home, Tim, is going to be in town next week for a college interview. The only time he can see me is Friday night, and we've planned to meet in the Pizza Palace around ten-thirty."

"And you need to escape for a few hours," Renée surmised.

"Exactly. And you guys have got to help me."

"We're experts at that," Ellen said.

Carrie gasped at the thought that anyone would attempt anything so risky. Smoking seemed tame after she heard the girls devise a scheme where they would switch rooms, allowing Hilary to be on the first floor, where it was easier to sneak out.

"Be sure and wear dark clothes," someone cautioned. "That way you can slip by Mr. Oslo, the security guard. It might be one of the times he's actually patroling the grounds and not dozing off."

"And if you are noticed, the best thing is to pretend you're a member of the faculty. Say 'Good evening' in your most offhand manner, and keep moving."

"Good evening," Hilary said in such a small voice that the group cracked up.

"That'll never do!" another girl said. "You must learn to project."

"But how?" Hilary asked miserably.

"I'll be happy to show you. Come to my room later tonight and we'll practice. I'll have you sounding like the oldest member of the faculty in no time."

"Thanks, guys," Hilary said, noticeably relieved. "With you all behind me, I know I can pull it off."

Carrie was more than ever conscious of the warm feeling generated by The Club. The members were really there to help one another, and she was proud to be one of them.

Before they were dismissed, Renée told them the next meeting would take place before breakfast the following Wednesday in the Ping-Pong room in Franklin. "Be there promptly at seven."

Carrie was surprised that there were no objections to the early hour. It was evident that The Club meant more to its members than an extra hour's sleep.

"Why the Ping-Pong room?" Jennifer asked.

"Because it's in the cellar. No one will hear us and not a soul will be around at that hour."

The girls noisily commended the reason, and Ellen raised her hands and told them to Ssshh. "We must break up now, so please be quiet while I open the door and make sure no one is around."

Then she slipped out of the shed and returned almost immediately. "Coast is clear, but don't make too much noise. Also, better straggle out in twos so we're not conspicuous."

Kim motioned to Carrie, and they left together. When they were a safe distance from the shed, Kim said, "You were a terrific sport about the smoking."

"I wasn't sure if I'd survive."

"I'll be happy to give you some private lessons, free of charge."

Carrie giggled. "I think I could use some."

"Didn't I tell you The Club would be fun?"

"You sure did. And the girls are so great."

"I think we'll be friends with a lot of them."

"I think so, too, but I'll never have a better friend than you, Kim."

The rest of the week all anyone could talk about was the mixer, which would take place at eight o'clock in the girls' dining room on Saturday night. Carrie now thought of her life in terms of Before Mark and After Mark. Before Mark she would have been uninterested in conversations about a dance, but now she hung on every detail.

On Friday after their last class, Carrie went along on a

shopping expedition with Kim, Ginger, and Nancy. Nancy had promised her folks that she wouldn't hole up in her room whenever there was a coed party. "Besides, even though I'm not interested in meeting anyone, I don't want to live like a hermit."

"Good thinking," Ginger said. "And it's a good excuse to buy something."

"That's how I feel," said Kim.

As Carrie listened to the others chattering about what they might buy, something went *click* in her head. Her father had never put any restrictions on how she spent her allowance, and it had never occurred to her to use it for anything except essentials. It wouldn't have been possible for her to make any extravagant purchases, but she was definitely in the mood to buy something frivolous.

"The best boutique in town is The Purple Planet," Nancy told her. "Their stuff is a little far out, though."

"Carrie could stand something far out," Ginger observed bluntly.

"What Ginger means is you're ready for something different." Kim wanted to soften Ginger's remark.

"I know what Ginger means," Carrie said with a chuckle, "and she happens to be a hundred percent right."

That set the tone for the shopping spree, and they were all in high spirits when they arrived at The Purple Planet. NO BARE FEET OR ICE CREAM said a sign in the window. It was a spacious, sleek shop, with several built-in racks of pants, skirts, and tops, and shelves loaded with sweaters. Nancy led the way past the glass case of jewelry toward the back of the store, and the girls zeroed in on the clothes.

A pretty young woman who looked like her auburn hair had been frizzed by an electric shock approached them. "Let me know when I can help you," she said, and moved away so that she wouldn't interfere with their browsing.

For the next half hour, the girls tried on outfits for one another. At first Carrie was self-conscious—almost afraid to try anything too exotic—but soon she was swept away with everyone else's enthusiasm. When she slithered into a bright yellow lycra leotard, Ginger let out a whoop.

"You've got to have that," she insisted, and everyone else agreed.

"I've never owned anything like this, and it's so skin-tight, I wouldn't be allowed at the mixer. It would just be a waste of money."

"You don't just wear the leotard, Carrie. You wear it with something," Ginger explained patiently, taking from the rack a flared skirt printed with small multicolored flowers.

"Try it on," Kim urged.

Carrie stepped into the skirt and twirled around.

"Sensational!" Ginger said. "Maybe I should be a fashion coordinator."

"I'd give anything to be tall and thin like you," Nancy groaned. "You inspire me to go on a crash diet."

"I saw a great poison-green overblouse for you," Ginger said. "Come with me and I'll show it to you."

When they had disappeared into a fitting room, Kim turned to Carrie. "What you're wearing is perfect," she said.

"I'm going to buy it." Carrie spoke with finality.

"Now all you need is some glitzy earrings."

"Who? Me? I don't think that's my style."

"It is now," Kim said smiling, and pulled Carrie by the arm toward the jewelry case.

"You haven't led me astray yet," Carrie said.

"And I never will," Kim assured her. "I never will."

Chapter 8

*T*he night of the mixer, the dorm buzzed with anticipation. The girls zipped in and out of one another's room asking opinions, borrowing things, wanting to see what everyone else was wearing. Carrie was caught up in the excitement and realized she had never looked forward to a party so much. As she trooped over to the dining hall with half of Ellsworth, the compliments flew back and forth. Carrie received more than her share, and the general consensus was that she looked terrific. She couldn't believe how much it meant to her.

The dining room had been transformed into a festive dance hall, festooned with crepe ribbons and balloons descending from the ceiling. Japanese lanterns provided the only light, which made the usual sterile atmosphere surprisingly romantic. The furniture had been pushed aside to make room for a dance area, except for a long table that boasted a banquet of junk food—a variety of chips and dips, sodas, popcorn, candy, and pastry. Music blasted out of the speakers strategically placed around the room, charging the air with electricity.

"It's hard to believe this is Adams," Nancy said as soon as they arrived.

"We'll be reminded soon enough," Ginger remarked, and tilted her head toward Ms. Calhoun, the girls' athletic coach, who everyone agreed must have been born with a lanyard and a whistle around her neck. There were a couple of male faculty members from the boys' school who were also chaperons, but it was clear that Coach was in charge.

Mark had been standing on the sidelines, close to the entrance. As soon as he saw Carrie, he bounded toward her and pulled her onto the dance area. The music was loud and fast, but Mark ignored the beat, and the two of them swayed gently together.

"If a man does not keep pace with his companions, perhaps it is because he hears a different drummer," Mark whispered in her ear.

"Let him step to the music which he hears, however measured or far away." Carrie finished the quote for him.

Mark stopped dancing and looked at Carrie with more admiration than ever. "You're the only person I know who could finish those lines."

"That's because Thoreau happens to be one of my favorite writers."

"I just can't believe it," Mark said, and again tightly encircled her with his arms.

While all the other couples bounced around, doing their own thing—they might as well have been dancing alone— Mark and Carrie covered less than one square foot of the floor. Then abruptly the volume was turned down and Ms. Calhoun blew her whistle until she had everyone's attention.

"Welcome, boys and girls. This is our first mixer of the year, and for those of you who are new, that's exactly what we want it to be—a mixer. None of this pairing up with one person all evening. The purpose is to circulate. Therefore, whenever I blow my whistle, I want you to change partners. Right now, I want you to dance with the person nearest to your left, naturally of the opposite sex."

Both Carrie and Mark were crestfallen. The last thing they wanted was to be separated.

"There must be some way to beat the system," Mark groaned.

"I hope so," Carrie said just as Max, who was at least half a head shorter than she, moved over to her.

"You're all mine," he said, putting his hand possessively on her shoulder.

Mark reluctantly released her. He was still looking at Carrie longingly when a girl with braces on her teeth and frizzy hair held her arms out to him.

"I'm Mary Jo. It's you and me," she piped up in a squeaky voice.

"Guess so." Mark didn't want to hurt her feelings, but he had trouble keeping a resigned note out of his voice.

The music started up again, and Carrie kept eye contact with Mark until Max spun her around and she lost sight of him. It wasn't easy to follow Max, who was more interested in showing off than he was in dancing. Then, when he executed some crazy maneuver all by himself so that his partner wasn't involved at all, Carrie just stood and watched despairingly.

She wasn't aware that Kim, who was dancing with one of her many admirers, noticed her. Kim understood immediately why Carrie looked so disgruntled and decided to do something about it. When there was another break, and Ms. Calhoun did her whistle number, Kim went into action. She sidled over to Renée and explained Carrie's dilemma.

"We can handle this," Renée said, and promptly enlisted the help of another S.N. member.

The word was passed along that Carrie and Mark wanted to be together. In order to make sure this would happen, the S.N. girls took turns dancing with Mark whenever the whistle blew. After a few minutes, so that the eagle-eyed coach wouldn't catch on, they would switch partners with Carrie and whomever she happened to be dancing with.

The first time this occurred, Carrie and Mark were delighted and perplexed. They thought it was a freakish accident. But after this happened five or six times, they saw a pattern emerge. Carrie knew The Club was behind it, but she couldn't let on.

Mark said, "I told you there was a way to beat the system. I think you must have some great friends who are making this happen."

"I do," Carrie said happily. "I didn't know until now how great."

Before the last set was played, Ms. Calhoun made an announcement.

"I think you all agree that this has been an enormously successful mixer. You may choose your partner for the last dance of the evening. I should warn you that I'm going to lower the speed and the decibel count of the music. After all, athletes, like horses, must be walked around and cooled off before being returned to the stable."

Everyone laughed and applauded. Then the music resumed, and Mark and Carrie glided across the floor as though they'd been dancing partners all their lives.

When Ms. Calhoun gave her final blast on her whistle and unplugged the stereo, Mark sighed. "I can't believe it's midnight."

"Me neither. It went so fast."

"At least there's tomorrow to look forward to."

"Tomorrow? What's happening?"

"We have rehearsal, and I'll see you. And maybe after we can go to the Frost Bite if you'd like."

"I'd like," Carrie said without hesitation.

They looked lovingly at each other, so much unsaid, until a voice boomed from across the room. It came from one of the chaperons, a relaxed and rumpled English teacher from the boys' school who always spoke in superlatives.

"Ahoy, Mark, it's the witching hour. You'll be locked in here, perhaps for eternity, if you don't leave now."

"Okay, Mr. Dempsey," Mark shouted back, trying not to show his embarrassment.

"Hurry up, Carrie," Ginger called from the doorway. "We're waiting for you."

"I think we're getting a message," Carrie said, and gave Mark's arm a meaningful squeeze before she hurried to catch up with her friends.

The girls chatted excitedly on the way back to their dorms. Everyone had something to say. "Did you dance with that guy Larry? He's got two left feet." "Can't be worse than Jason, who thinks dancing means placing his feet at regular intervals squarely on top of his partner's." "The food was the best part. I had three Baby Ruths and two Tabs. Maybe that's why I don't feel so good." "This guy Bob promised to call me. What should I do if he doesn't?" "Make some cutting remark next time you see him." "All my partners were nerds." "Mine were all cute."

The remarks swirled like smoke around Carrie, who was lost in her own private thoughts. She was glowing with the memory of being in Mark's arms.

"How were your partners, Carrie? Nerds or Cutes?" Kim asked mischievously.

Carrie looked blank until Kim touched her arm and repeated the question.

"You know the answer to that," Carrie said. "If it hadn't been for you . . ."

"We did the best we could." Kim lowered her voice. "Remember, S.N. now and forever."

"Now and forever," Carrie said, and the two of them smiled like Cheshire cats.

Chapter 9

*T*he next few weeks for Carrie were a combination of
hard academic work, orchestral rehearsals, special lab
projects, rapping with her friends, S.N. meetings, and
seeing Mark. Everything took on a special glow because of
him.

The two of them invented a game that turned an ordinary
activity into a romantic episode. They took a ride in a
rowboat and fantasized that they were in a gondola on a
canal in Venice; a ham sandwich shared in the orchard
became a picnic out of a Renoir painting; sipping a soda at
the Frost Bite had an aura of having cappuccino in an
outdoor café on the Left Bank in Paris. As the Thanksgiving
holiday approached, and they knew they would be apart for
five whole days, their imagination went wild—Mark was
off to the wars, Carrie was joining the Peace Corps, one of
them was a spy and had a mission overseas. They ended
these scenes collapsed in laughter.

The Wednesday before the holiday there was a mad
scramble in the dorms. Typically, everyone had waited until

after her last class to start packing, and then there were the farewells, which were fraught with drama. Some of the girls actually broke into tears. Carrie, who earlier might have scoffed at such an outward display of emotion, was totally sympathetic. Strangely enough, although she couldn't wait to see her father, she now felt that Adams was home.

When Mark walked her to the bus stop with her suitcase, he sensed how she felt. As they waited for the bus that would take her to the airport, he tried to cheer her up.

"Remember, I'm not really going off to the wars, and you're not joining the Peace Corps, and neither of us is a spy on an overseas mission."

"I know," she said, chuckling. "And it's only five days."

"Then what's bothering you?"

"I just know I'm so different from when I left Butler. I'm not sure what my father will think."

"He'll think you're wonderful," Mark said.

Then the bus came into view, and although it was against all the rules, he boldly kissed her good-bye in front of the other passengers.

"You've changed too," she said softly, as she saw the amused looks surrounding them.

"And what do you think of me?" he asked nervously.

"I think you're wonderful."

After Carrie boarded the bus, she took a window seat so she could wave to Mark until she could no longer see him. It was the first time in weeks that she was alone, and she looked forward to a few hours on the plane to adjust to being in her hometown.

In spite of Mark's assurance, Carrie still had apprehensions about seeing Len. She was wearing the same navy blue suit he last saw her in but had brightened her appearance with a red scarf, a long golden chain, and dangling earrings. Her makeup was expertly applied, and her hair was different too. Carrie had recently experimented with new hairstyles, and she now wore her hair pulled back with tortoiseshell combs. It was a much more sophisticated look than the bobby pins she had used for the sole purpose of keeping her hair out of her eyes.

Shortly before the plane touched down, Carrie entertained the idea of running into the lavatory, washing her face, and removing her jewelry. But she decided that would be cowardly. Her father would have to accept the new Carrie.

She tried to ignore the butterflies of anxiety as the plane taxied toward the air terminal. Then she yanked her carry-on suitcase from the overhead storage space, straightened her shoulders, and descended the steps of the plane.

Len was waiting for her at the receiving gate. She ran toward him and dropped her bag, and he hugged her to him. When he stepped back to look at her, there was a bemused expression on his face.

"Carrie," he said, "you look so . . . so different."

"How do I look?" she asked, the butterflies fluttering wildly. "It's only been eight weeks and I couldn't have aged that much."

"That's not what I mean. You look . . . you look terrific."

"Thanks, Dad." She sighed with relief and planted an affectionate kiss on his cheek.

Len picked up her bag, thrust his arm around her shoulder, and guided her toward the parking lot. When they got settled in the old blue Chevvy, Len said, "The only plans I've made are for tomorrow, when we're going to Aunt Mary's. A couple of your friends from Butler called and mentioned something about a party on Saturday. I told them you'd be home tonight. And I thought Friday we might go for a pizza and movie."

"Sounds great. I do have to spend some time finishing a

paper on D. H. Lawrence's *Sons and Lovers*. Mr. Benson gave us the assignment weeks ago, and it's due next Monday."

"One thing I've never worried about was you not doing your homework."

"I still find time for that," Carrie said without thinking.

Len raised his eyebrows and glanced at her sideways. "I suppose you're busy with orchestra and lab, right?"

"Right," Carrie answered quickly.

"I can remember myself from college days that much of my free time was having what we called bull sessions and you call rapping."

"That too," Carrie said.

Len tactfully waited for his daughter to go on. He sensed that she had something else to say, but he didn't want to press.

Carrie wasn't sure herself why she was so hesitant to come right out and tell her father about Mark. She wanted him to know but was afraid he might not like the idea. But not telling him was worse.

"There's another reason I'm so busy, Dad."

"What's that?"

Carrie took a deep breath. "There's this boy, Mark Newman, and he takes up a lot of my time."

Now it was Carrie's turn to wait. It seemed to take forever for Len to react, and for a moment she thought he hadn't heard her. She stared straight ahead, as though she were responsible for watching the road.

"Is he your boyfriend?" he asked finally.

"I guess you might call him that." Carrie looked at him then and saw he was smiling.

"Do you want to tell me about him?"

"Sure do," she exclaimed, and for the rest of the ride home she bubbled on about Mark.

"Sounds like Superman," Len said when she finished.

"In a way he is," Carrie said seriously. Then she realized her father was teasing her and she managed to laugh at herself.

"If you like him, I'm sure I will," Len told her.

"Thanks, Dad," Carrie said.

Carrie relaxed totally then, and the last of the butterflies disappeared. The two hurdles she had worried so much about had been successfully crossed: Len approved her new style, and he had accepted the fact that she had a boyfriend.

As soon as they set foot in the house, the phone rang. Carrie picked up the receiver in the kitchen and settled down on the kitchen stool to talk. It was Betty, an old classmate from Butler High. Betty was slightly ditzy, boy crazy, and a very good writer. She and Carrie had been ninth-grade cub reporters together, but they didn't have much else in common. Betty had almost given up on trying to get Carrie to be more sociable.

They chatted for a long time about everything they'd been doing, and Betty filled Carrie in on all the gossip. If she was surprised at how interested Carrie was, she didn't let on. Then she invited her to a "bring a dessert" party for Saturday night, fully prepared to hear some excuse as to why she couldn't come.

"I'd love to," Carrie said without hesitation.

After they'd settled the details as to time and what dessert Carrie would make—"anything as long as it's chocolate and fabulous"—Carrie hung up.

She was still sitting on the kitchen stool, frowning, when Len came in a few minutes later. He went to the fridge and got out some cheese and crackers and a bottle of wine that he had chilled.

"To celebrate your homecoming," he said, holding up the bottle.

Carrie nodded her head distractedly.

"What's wrong?" Len asked. "You look like you've been asked to solve the nuclear disarmament problem."

Carrie laughed out loud. "Not quite. I'm just wondering what I should wear to the party Saturday night."

"Just like a woman," Len observed.

"That's what I am," Carrie said with a touch of pride.

Len concentrated on opening the bottle of wine and said in a soft voice, "My little girl has grown up."

Carrie felt like a royal princess when she visited her aunt and uncle. Mary, as usual, bemoaned the fact that she never saw enough of her. Ken, who was always ebullient, told her, "You look radiant. You must be in love."

Carrie blushed and was grateful that her little cousins chose that moment to get into a fistfight over who was going to show her their new tree house.

"Why don't we go together?" Carrie said, breaking them up and taking each one by the hand.

They momentarily simmered down as they traipsed into the backyard. But the rest of the afternoon they vied with each other for Carrie's attention. Carrie was amused and flattered at the same time.

After stuffing themselves on the traditional Thanksgiving dinner, from roast turkey and all the trimmings to three kinds of pies, everyone helped with the dishes. Then the boys went out to play, Len and Ken watched the football game on television, and Mary beckoned Carrie into the bedroom.

Mary loved buying gifts for Carrie, and on every family occasion gave her something special. This time she presented her with a large box wrapped in silver foil.

"It's different," Mary warned. "Not your usual boarding school outfit." She was sensitive to Carrie's need to dress conservatively, and she knew she was taking a chance.

Carrie carefully opened the box and removed a mound of

tissue paper. She pulled out an electric blue blouse banded with black leather, and a narrow black leather skirt.

"Wow," Carrie breathed, "this is sensational."

"You really like it?" Mary asked nervously.

"I love it," Carrie said, slipping out of her clothes and trying them on.

"It fits perfectly!" Mary cried. "I hope you can use it."

'It's just what I need for the party Saturday night, and there are these mixers at school."

"Mixers? What are they?"

For the next hour, Carrie told her aunt all about school, her classes, her friends, and even about Mark. She no longer felt she had to be secretive about him. The one important aspect of Adams that she would never reveal was S.N. The Club meant so much to her, and upon pain of death she wouldn't betray the members' unspoken vow of secrecy.

The next day passed very quickly, with Carrie preparing a chocolate icebox cake, working on her paper, and making some calls to a few of her Butler High classmates. Although she was closer to Kim than to any other girl, she had learned from her the value of having a wide circle of friends.

As Carrie soaked in a bubble bath before the party—a rare treat after sharing a community bathroom—she mused about these things. Kim was responsible for so much that had happened to her, and she wondered if she could ever repay her. She even attributed the fact that she was less uptight about going to a Butler party than ever before to Kim's influence. And she had absolutely no qualms about wearing her new slinky skirt and top.

Her father dropped her off at Betty's split-level house on his way to playing bridge at his friends', the Manfelds.

"Have a great time, honey," he said as she got out of the car, balancing the cake. "What time should I collect you?"

"Someone will probably walk me home," Carrie said confidently.

"Probably," Len managed to say as Carrie turned toward the house. He shook his head, remembering in the past how Carrie had always made sure that Len picked her up at a specific time.

Carrie rang the doorbell and Tony, one of Butler High's superjocks, opened the door. For a few seconds he couldn't seem to place her.

"You," he shouted, "it's you!"

"Me Carrie, you Tony," she said, laughing.

"I didn't recognize you. I mean you look so . . . so good."

"Is that supposed to be a compliment?"

Tony was flustered, and started to say, "I mean there's something about you . . ."

Betty came over at that moment, pushed Tony aside, greeted Carrie enthusiastically, and yelled at Tony to close the door.

"Tony has designated himself official doorman," Betty explained to Carrie, "but he doesn't understand the purpose is to let people in, not keep them standing in the cold."

"I'm new at this," Tony said, and motioned Carrie to come in.

Betty took the cake from her and waited while Tony helped her off with her coat and hung it in the hall closet.

"Love your leather," Betty said as Carrie followed her into the dining room and placed the cake on the table already laden with luscious desserts.

"Thanks, Betty. I think your outfit is terrific." Betty was poured into a red stretch jumpsuit that showed off her twenty-inch waist.

Betty tilted her head in surprise but didn't have to say anything. Carrie had never evinced any interest in clothes, and certainly never bothered to comment on what anyone was wearing. She was getting used to the idea that everyone thought she had changed, and enjoying the effect.

"You can tell where the action is," Betty said. "Just follow your ears."

Carrie did just that and they ended up in the family room, which was vibrating with sound. There were three distinct groups, besides the dancers, in the large pine-panelled room. One group hovered around a soft-drink bar set up at one end, another warmed themselves at the wood-burning fireplace at the other, and a third stood around the built-in stereo unit.

Carrie headed for the bar, a reflex action that guaranteed that she didn't look as if she was waiting for someone to ask her to dance. But she had barely taken two steps when several kids ran up to her and started asking a zillion questions. "What's it like at boarding school?" "Do you remember Mrs. Zorn? She's our homeroom teacher. Yuck!" "How long will you be in town?"

In the middle of all this, Tony zoomed into the room and landed next to Carrie. "I've just resigned as doorman," he announced, "and I've promoted myself to Social Director. I now take it upon myself to show our visiting royalty a good time."

With that, he whisked Carrie onto the dance floor and whirled her around.

Carrie was amazed that Tony was paying any attention to her at all. He'd always been totally indifferent to her, and the feeling was mutual. Tony had been linked, at one time or another, with every cheerleader on the squad. Carrie never came close to being that type, and she knew it.

These thoughts raced through her mind as Tony danced her around the room. Her opinion of Tony hadn't changed, but he was a terrific dancer, and she found herself getting into it.

"Where've you been all my life?" Tony asked.

"Well, until last year I was a student at Butler," Carrie answered coolly.

Tony wasn't sure how to take this. He was used to having girls flip over him, and for the second time that night Carrie's response put him off balance.

"I think I may have missed something," he said after a pause.

"Like what?" Carrie asked innocently.

"Like you," Tony answered.

Carrie wondered about his sincerity but really didn't care if he was handing her a line or not. She wasn't the least bit interested. She was spared having to say anything, because just then Andy, who was a cartoonist for the Butler High paper and an old friend—not the least bit romantically—caught Carrie's eye. Andy was short, wore glasses, and was known for his sarcastic wit.

"Excuse me," Carrie said and moved toward Andy, leaving Tony more baffled than ever.

Andy gave her a big hello and then suggested they get a Tab. They threaded their way through the crowd to the bar and helped themselves.

"I want to hear all about Adams," Andy said. "I'm not much for dancing . . . I'm more into pillow talk. Shall we take advantage of that seating arrangement over there?" He pointed to a group of floor pillows in the far corner of the room.

"Let's go," Carrie said.

Once they had settled down, Andy proceeded to quiz her, and Carrie found she was delighted to talk about her new school. They were so involved in conversation that Carrie didn't notice Tony until he was practically on top of them.

"This is a party, not a gab fest. Don't you want to dance, Carrie?"

"In a few minutes," Carrie said, not wanting to be rude.

"That's okay," Andy said amicably, getting to his feet. Then he reached for Carrie's hand, pulled her up, pushed her toward the floor, and held her in a fox-trot position.

"That's not what I had in mind," Tony called after them, and couldn't help laughing.

Carrie laughed too, appreciating that Tony was a good enough sport to see the humor in the situation. It didn't bother her that Andy was not only short but also uncoordinated. She enjoyed talking to him. The feeling was reciprocated, because when Tony approached a short time later, Andy said to Carrie in a low voice, "This guy's persistent, but we're not done yet. Can I walk you home?"

"I'd like that," Carrie said.

Tony must have overheard them, because the first thing he said was, "He beat me to it. I was hoping *I* could walk you home."

"Too late," Carrie said, grateful that she had a legitimate excuse to refuse. She knew Tony's reputation, and the last thing she wanted was a wrestling match.

A number of other boys cut in and Carrie didn't concern herself all evening about not having a partner. In fact, she barely had a chance to sample the tempting desserts before someone asked her to dance.

It was after midnight when Betty's parents appeared, a subtle way of saying the party was over. There were a few audible sighs, but everyone graciously took the hint.

It was hard to explain, because Carrie really missed Mark and he had been in the back of her mind all evening, but when she thanked Betty, she could truthfully say, "I can't believe I had such a good time!"

Chapter 10

Carrie was in the clouds in every sense on the trip back to Virginia. She had wonderful memories of her mini-vacation in Butler. It had surpassed all her expectations, and now she could look forward to seeing all her friends, especially Kim and Mark and members of The Club.

The first thing she did after dumping her bags in her room was rush downstairs to call Mark's dorm from the one private phone housed in a converted closet on the main floor of Ellsworth.

"Mission accomplished," she said conspiratorially when she finally reached Mark.

"You delivered the tapes?"

"As planned."

"No interference?"

"None."

Carrie couldn't keep up the secret agent act and burst out, "Mark, how are you?"

"Better, now that we're in the same county. Those five days seemed like centuries without you."

"I missed you, too."

"When can I see you?"

"It's too late now. What about tomorrow?"

"Before breakfast?"

"I'll meet you on the hockey field. No one in their right mind will be there at that hour."

"Seven-thirty. You're on!"

Carrie left the phone room smiling to herself, and brushed by someone waiting to get in. She didn't realize who it was until Nancy shouted, "Hey, Carrie, how about saying hello?"

Carrie turned around and apologized. "I'm sorry, Nancy. I didn't see you. I was just talking to Mark."

"It figures," Nancy said understandingly. "I'm calling Sam now."

"Didn't you just see him?"

"That was more than three hours ago."

"I know how it is."

Then Carrie climbed the stairs to the third floor, intending to see Kim, and was surprised that her door was closed. She rapped gently at first, and when there was no response, more forcefully. Still no answer.

Carrie put her ear to the door, and was sure she heard muffled crying.

"I'm coming in," she warned, and impulsively opened the door.

She was astounded to see Kim stretched out on her bed, her head buried under her pillow.

"What's wrong?" Carrie asked in alarm. She ran over to Kim and sat beside her on the bed.

"Everything," Kim sobbed.

"Come on, Kim. It can't be that bad."

"If you call losing my scholarship not bad, then maybe you're right."

"What are you talking about?" Carrie reached for a couple of tissues from a box that was on the floor and handed them to her. "Everything was fine when you left, and you couldn't have broken too many rules since you're back. Now please, try and make some sense."

Kim sat up and blew her nose. "You don't understand," she groaned. "It's my paper on *Rabbit, Run* for Benson."

"What about it?"

"It's due tomorrow and I haven't even finished reading the last fifty pages."

"Maybe, if you have a good reason, he'll give you an extension," Carrie suggested.

"He won't." Kim sniffed. "Don't you remember? He told us he was doing us a big favor by letting us have until after Thanksgiving to hand it in."

"I do remember that. . . ." Carrie frowned, and for the moment couldn't think of anything comforting to say.

"Don't you see what it means? You know that because we're on scholarships, we have to keep up our academic standing. If I get an F in English, I might as well pack my bags. Can you imagine how disappointed my parents will be? And the worse thing is, I don't want to leave Adams. Oh Carrie, what's going to happen to me?" Kim was overcome with another spasm of sobbing.

Carrie put her arms around her, letting her cry on her shoulder, and she finally quieted down.

"Where are your notes on what you've read so far?" Carrie asked.

Kim looked more distressed than ever, if possible, but Carrie wasn't prepared for her answer.

"I left them at home," she murmured.

"You left them at home," Carrie echoed, trying to keep calm.

"I brought them with me because I wanted to type them

up, but I kept putting it off. There were a zillion parties—even breakfast bashes. I didn't want to miss anything . . . and now I'm going to miss everything." The tears streamed down her cheeks again.

Carrie stood up and started pacing around the room. "Desperate needs call for desperate measures," she stated.

"What do you mean?" Kim asked meekly.

"I mean that it's almost six o'clock now. If we work around the clock we can come up with something. You won't get your usual A, but you won't get an F, either."

"But I haven't even finished the book," Kim whimpered.

"You haven't, but I have," Carrie said triumphantly. "John Updike happens to be one of my favorite authors. I can tell you the ending."

"You mean it?" Kim eyes brightened, and she almost smiled.

"I mean it," Carrie said. "But we've got to get started right away."

"Where'll we go?"

"We'll have to let Ginger and Nancy in on it. I'm sure Ginger won't mind spending the night here, and then we can use my room."

"That's a fantastic idea. Do you mind if we skip dinner?"

"Course not. It's probably Adams' Welcome Back speciality—sautéed lambs' tails. We can arrange with someone in The Club to loan us the Hot Pot. We'll need coffee to keep us going."

"Oh Carrie," Kim exclaimed, jumping up, "you're saving my life!"

"It hasn't happened yet," Carrie cautioned. "I'll go fix things with Ginger, and you corner Nancy if she ever gets off the phone. I'll tell Renée and Ellen what's happening. They're experts at this sort of thing."

"If I wasn't so scared, I'd think this was kind of exciting."

"If you like Grade B movies," Carrie quipped and hurried out of the room.

Within fifteen minutes, everything was sorted out as far as the rooming arrangement; Renée's aid had been enlisted for borrowing S.N.'s illegal Hot Pot; Ellen said that she would have herself and several other club members keep Mrs. Gore engaged in conversation after dinner until well after Lights Out. The housemother was known to make a friendly visit to each girl's room after a school holiday, and Ellen warned that Mrs. Gore's good intentions could blow the whole scheme. And finally, Carrie made another call to Mark to cancel their before-breakfast date.

"I'll make it up to you," she said.

Then she made him promise not to say anything to Kim about the change in plans, because she didn't want her to be any more upset. Carrie explained Kim's panic and told him how she wanted to do everything in her power to help her. "I've never seen Kim so unhinged."

"I understand," Mark said, "and I admire you more every day."

With Mark's support, Carrie was more energized than ever. But when she returned to her room, she saw that Kim had flopped down in the easy chair and was staring into space. Apparently, in Carrie's brief absence, Kim had been overwhelmed again with the prospect of failing. Carrie knew she couldn't allow for any weakness on Kim's part. She sat down at her desk, turned to face Kim, and spoke firmly.

"Okay, Kim, let's get started. Tell me as much of the novel as you remember and what it means."

Kim sat up straight, blinked several times, and with what

Carrie viewed as a superhuman effort, rattled off some disconnected thoughts about the story.

"All I know," Kim said finally, aware that she'd presented a very muddled version, "is that the main character, Rabbit, had been a star basketball player as a teenager and found everything in his life after that was pretty miserable."

"That's right," Carrie said. "But you left out the main point, which is how Rabbit is constantly running away from responsibility."

"Sort of like me," Kim wailed, still suffering from the mess she'd gotten herself into.

"Stop worrying about you," Carrie snapped. "The reason we're here is to write a paper. Now take down some notes." She took a large yellow legal-sized pad and pen from her desk and handed them to her. Then she proceeded to tell her the plot, emphasizing the features that revealed Rabbit's immature behavior. When she was finished, she insisted that Kim tell the story back to her in her own words in order to make sure she had it straight.

"That's good," Carrie said with relief. "Now write it up."

"Me?" Kim said, as though she'd been asked to scale Mount Everest.

"You, you have to," Carrie said in a stern voice. But when she saw the look of panic on Kim's face, she added, "I'll be here to hold your hand and keep us both fueled up with coffee."

"I have to," Kim groaned, and slowly began writing.

Carrie realized at that moment that their roles had been reversed. Kim had been the natural leader, and without being bossy had told Carrie how to dress, what makeup to use, why she should join The Club. Carrie had acquiesced, hesitantly at first, but then was very grateful. Now she had an opportunity to pay her back.

They worked nonstop for hours, only pausing to refill their coffee mugs. Kim scribbled on a dozen sheets of paper and gave them to Carrie as she went along. Carrie corrected the spelling and made a few suggestions, which Kim readily accepted.

It was after midnight when Kim announced, "I can't go on." Her face was still blotchy from crying, and her eyes were bleary.

Carrie didn't want to press her any further. "Why don't you catch a nap, Kim, and I'll wake you in a couple of hours?"

"Okay," Kim said, giving the pad and pen to Carrie. "These final pages are beginning to look like hieroglyphics."

Then she dragged herself over to Ginger's bed, fell on top of it, didn't bother to get out of her clothes or get under the covers, and was sound asleep in seconds.

Carrie mustered all her strength, knowing she might have to work the rest of the night alone. She bolted down another cup of black coffee and started typing. After two hours, she looked hopefully at Kim, thinking she would wake her up. But Kim was sleeping so soundly, she didn't have the heart. She continued typing until four o'clock in the morning, only taking a break to raid Ginger's supply of candy bars. When the final page was completed, she collapsed on her bed and fell into an exhausted sleep.

When the seven o'clock bell rang, Kim awoke but had the feeling she was still dreaming. This wasn't her room, she wasn't in her night shirt, and she was lying on top of a strange bed. It took her several minutes to remember where she was and why. Then, in a flash, it all came back to her.

The last thing she recalled was that she'd fallen asleep with her clothes on and left Carrie working.

Kim saw a small pile of paper on Carrie's desk and leapt off the bed to investigate. Her eyes shone with tears as she thumbed through the neatly typed paper.

"I can't believe it," she cried. "I just can't believe it."

"You say something?" Carrie croaked, coming out of a deep sleep.

"You did it!" Kim shouted. "You did it! You got me through the worst day of my life!"

"We're best friends, aren't we?" Carrie said simply.

"You know it!" Kim said. "And you saved my life."

Chapter 11

A week later at the end of the class Mr. Benson returned the papers. Carrie was delighted to see that she had received an A with the comment "Excellent indeed!" in the margin. But that wasn't what concerned her. What she was really anxious about was Kim's mark, and she waited impatiently for her in the hall.

"Well?" Carrie said, as soon as she saw her.

"Well what?" Kim answered evenly.

"Did you pass?"

Kim couldn't hold out, so she flashed her paper at Carrie and broke into her headlight smile.

"B-plus!" Carrie exclaimed. "That's fantastic."

"I learned my lesson the hard way, and I'm going to be so-o-o-o good now. I'll never let anything like this happen again."

"It wasn't so bad."

"If you don't mind starving and staying up all night."

"That was the least of it."

Kim picked up on what Carrie had let slip. "You mean there was something else?"

Carrie frowned thoughtfully. "I wasn't going to say anything, but now that it's over I can tell you. The worst thing was I had to break an early-bird date with Mark. We'd been apart for five whole days, you know."

"Oh Carrie, I feel awful."

"You shouldn't. He understood perfectly. Besides, I did it for myself."

"What do you mean?"

"Adams wouldn't be the same for me without you. And I plan to make it up to Mark."

"How?"

"Do something exciting, like meet him after Lights Out."

"You're not serious, Carrie."

"Yes I am. I thought Heather was crazy when she snuck out after curfew to meet her boyfriend, but now I think it was really gutsy."

They were halfway down the corridor, and Kim stopped dead in her tracks. "What are you thinking of?"

"Something romantic, like meeting him in the orchard at four in the morning."

"What on earth for?"

"To see the sunrise."

"You're not kidding."

"Of course I'm not."

"But you'll be thrown out if you're discovered."

"It turned out fine for Heather."

"I know, but it's a terrible chance you're taking."

"You used to call me a worrywart, Kim, remember?"

"I do, but you better think twice. This could end in disaster."

"I'll take all the necessary precautions, and The Club will stand behind me."

"I know that . . . but . . ." The warning bell sounded and Kim said, "We better split now or we'll wind up on penalty crew for being late for class."

"A minor violation," Carrie teased.

"Maybe, but after what I've been through I don't want to mess around with breaking rules."

"Before you go, Kim, will you tell me just one thing?"

"Sure."

"Can I count on you to help me in the Carrie Caper?"

Kim shrugged her shoulders resignedly. "What can I say, Carrie? You're my best friend and I owe you."

The next meeting of The Club took place in the furnace room. The heat was almost overpowering, but at least it was safe. One problem was that they had to forgo smoking.

"We might have an explosion," Renée explained, "and that wouldn't do much for our secrecy."

"Or for Adams," Ellen added.

The main order of business was to discuss S.N.'s Christmas party, which would be a combination meeting and celebration of the new members' senior status in The Club.

"There's no doubt in my mind that our junior members— Kim, Pam, Jennifer, and Carrie—will successfully breeze through the initiation rite," Renée said. "Then they'll be presented with The Club's pin, which is three 'see no evil, hear no evil, speak no evil' monkeys. It has no distinguishing S.N. features, so that you can wear it without having to make explanations."

"What a brilliant idea!" Pam said, and the other juniors expressed their enthusiasm for becoming full-fledged members.

Then Renée routinely asked if there were any special requests, and Carrie promptly stood up.

"I need help," she began. "I'm going to meet my boyfriend in the orchard next Thursday and watch the sunrise."

There was a pleased murmur of approval, along with some amused looks and raised eyebrows. Carrie was the last person in the world anyone expected to attempt anything so bold.

"That's the spirit!" Ellen said encouragingly.

"How do I do it?" Carrie asked.

"It's easy," Heather offered. "The important thing is to get past Mr. Oslo. The night I went into town, he was half asleep in the guard booth and I slipped right by him. Coming back was a different story."

"What happened?" Kim asked. She was unable hide the fear in her voice.

"I had to pull the 'I'm faculty' bit. My heart was in my throat, but he fell for it."

"You were lucky," Kim said.

"Not lucky, skillful," Carrie countered. "If I'm aware of the dangers, I'll be prepared."

"What if something unforeseen happens—like you break a leg climbing out of the window?"

"Don't be a spoilsport, Kim," Renée said.

Kim was chagrined and decided to shut up. She thought maybe she was being overly cautious.

"The important thing is not to panic," Ellen advised.

"No danger of that. If worse comes to worst, and I'm caught, I can always say I was sleepwalking."

Everyone, except Kim, thought that was funny.

Then the experienced members told Carrie what she must do: wear clothes that would act as camouflage; arrange her bed covers so that it looked as if the bed were occupied;

swear her roommate to secrecy; and don't let anyone else know what's happening.

"It's very important that you have someone help you through the first-floor bathroom window. It's not too much of a drop, but the window must be closed once you leave. Mrs. Gore hates the cold, and if the temperature suddenly drops, she might get up to investigate. I don't have to remind you that the accomplice in crime is equally guilty. Any volunteers?"

Kim's hand shot up. Even though she didn't approve, she thought it was the least she could do for Carrie.

Carrie smiled at her appreciatively and gave her the thumbs-up sign.

Before the meeting was dismissed, Carrie was treated like an astronaut preparing for a flight in space. Then the crowd dispersed, and Carrie waited for Kim to leave the furnace room. Kim was unusually quiet as they headed for the third floor, and Carrie tried to reassure her.

"A lot of kids have done this. I'm not the first."

"I know, Carrie, but you've got to remember what's at stake."

"If you're really afraid, I'll get someone else to help me out the window."

"Don't be ridiculous," Kim said, with a bittersweet smile. "If you get kicked out of Adams, I'm going with you."

That night Carrie told her roommate about the escapade she was about to pull off.

"I'm proud of you," Ginger said. "I thought you were so proper when I first met you, but I'm beginning to look like the square one around here. Before you know it, you'll be horseback riding."

"That's not a bad idea," Carrie said, chuckling.

"Are you sure you've got every detail worked out?"

"I hope so. I'm going to wear jeans and a navy blue sweater so that I blend with the night; you'll cover for me if by some remote chance someone drops in our room; and Kim is going to help me out the window and then make sure it's closed."

"Kim's the perfect partner in crime."

"Yep," Carrie said, not wanting to dwell on the fact that her best friend had given her such a hard time.

"What about Mark?" Ginger asked.

"It's a lot easier for him. Because he's an upperclassman, he can get a late pass to the computer room or the science lab. From there, it's easy for him to slip out."

"How did you manage to think of everything? It's like you had some guiding light."

"It is," Carrie said truthfully. Upon penalty of death, she would never reveal the source of her advice.

"Well, you better get some sleep now. You're going to need all your strength for this stunt." Then she added thoughtfully, "I can't believe you're the same Carrie Gordon from Butler, Kansas."

"Me either," Carrie said, and dozed off with a smile on her lips.

Thursday night twenty minutes before Lights Out Kim dropped in on Carrie and Ginger. She tried not to appear nervous but her thin voice betrayed her.

"Let's synchronize our watches. I'll be at the window at three-forty-five A.M. Lucky I have an internal alarm clock so I won't bother Nancy."

"Great," Carrie said. "I'll arrive five minutes ahead so that no one hears the padding of two sets of feet."

"And I'll fix Carrie's bed as soon as she's gone so that it looks like there's still a body in it," Ginger told them.

"All systems go!" Carrie sang out.

"Roger!" Ginger exclaimed.

Kim held up her hands with her fingers crossed and silently backed out. When she got to her room, Nancy was curled up in bed, so absorbed in writing in her diary that she didn't notice how jumpy her roommate was. When the final bell rang, Kim told Nancy that she was going to study under the covers.

"I never thought I'd live to see the day you did the flashlight routine, Kim. That all-night paper ordeal must have scared you."

"It sure did," Kim said and let it go at that. It wasn't a lie and it was a good explanation for why she was so unglued.

Kim tossed fitfully all night, kept waking up and glancing at the digital clock on her desk, and was actually grateful when it was time for her to go into action. As quietly as possible, she got out of bed, put on her robe and sneakers— they made less noise than slippers—and crept out of the room and down the stairs.

Carrie, dressed according to plan, was already in the bathroom and had unlocked the window. She looked more as if she were about to take an early-morning run than have an illegal tryst on the campus.

"You're right on time," Carrie said in a normal tone.

"Ssshh," Kim hissed. "Mrs. Gore is on this floor."

"Okay, okay." Carrie lowered her voice, humoring her.

"How far is the drop?" Kim asked.

"About six feet."

Kim moved toward the window and peered out. "More like eight."

"Whatever . . . I'm going to do it. Here goes."

Carrie swung her legs over the ledge and hesitated briefly.

"Good luck," Kim whispered.

"Thanks, Kim. And don't forget to close the window."
Then she leapt down and landed with a dull thud.

Kim leaned out the window, barely able to see Carrie in
the darkness. "Are you all right?" she said.

"I'm fine," Carrie answered. Then there was a rustling
sound and she disappeared into the night.

Kim, robot-like, carefully closed the window, relocked
it, and returned to her room. As she crawled under the
covers, she told herself there was nothing more for her to
do. The first phase of the operation had been successfully
completed. There was no going back. If Carrie was lucky,
Kim would have to admit how foolish she'd been to be so
fearful. If not . . . She couldn't bear to think about the
consequences, and mercifully she finally fell asleep.

Carrie felt lighthearted, daring, intoxicated by the night
air. She and some of the S.N. members had carefully
designed her route. As planned, she stayed close to the
buildings for as long as possible. When she arrived at the
last one, she steeled herself for the next obstacle. The most
hazardous part was upon her. She had to cross thirty feet of
exposed lawn, where she would be silhouetted against the
sky.

She took several deep breaths, crouched down close to
the ground, raced across the grass, and reached the edge of
the orchard, gasping but victorious. Then she wended her
way through the trees, heading toward the middle of the
grove, which she and Mark had designated as their meeting
place.

"Who is that?" a voice croaked. It was unmistakably Mr.
Oslo.

Carrie was stunned. She was next to a large evergreen,
and froze to the spot. What was Mr. Oslo doing in the
orchard? He was known to patrol the grounds, making sure

no unauthorized people came through the gate, but he'd never been known to cruise the orchard.

Carrie wouldn't allow herself to panic, because then all would be lost. Instead, she took stock of the situation. The moon was out, but the branches of the trees diffused the light. That was to her advantage.

Her hopes of escaping discovery increased when she heard Mr. Oslo say, "Is anybody there?" That meant he hadn't seen her. Then she heard a rattling sound, followed by a glaring beam of light. It seemed to Carrie that Mr. Oslo must be using a thousand-kilowatt flashlight.

Carrie desperately reviewed the response she would make if Mr. Oslo saw her, and her heart sank. She could never get away with saying, "I'm faculty." It was one thing to be returning from town, as Heather had done, and get away with it, especially because Heather had been wearing a skirt. But what sane faculty member would be dressed in blue jeans and wandering around the orchard at night?

Carrie had almost stopped breathing and didn't know if she was feeling heady from lack of oxygen or the impossible situation she'd gotten herself into. When the arc of light made circles around her, she instinctively bent her head so that the light wouldn't reflect off her face.

"Anybody there?" Mr. Olso repeated, and pointed the flashlight in all directions. He waited then, obviously listening for a sound.

Carrie wasn't sure if she could keep still much longer. Her legs were stiff from staying in one position, and her chest was beginning to hurt. She was ready to surrender when there was a crunching of leaves, the flashlight was turned off, and Mr. Oslo muttered to himself, "Must be some wild animal who likes a moonlight stroll as much as I do."

Carrie almost toppled over with relief, but she kept her

wits about her and waited until she could see him ambling across the open lawn. Then she scrambled to the center of the grove as fast as she could and fell into Mark's arms.

"You made it," he said. "You're five minutes late, and I was beginning to worry."

"Only five minutes? It was more like a lifetime."

"What happened?"

"I practically bumped into Mr. Oslo. I came within a hair of being seen."

"Oh, Carrie, was it worth it?"

"Every minute of it, Mark. This whole idea was mine and I wouldn't disappoint you again."

"You're really something," Mark said, and hugged her close.

Chapter 12

*W*atching the sunrise with Mark was every bit as exhilarating as Carrie had anticipated. Except for the hairy minutes avoiding Mr. Oslo, everything had gone without a hitch. In retrospect, Carrie believed that even that near miss enhanced the excitement of her caper.

Mark and Carrie waited until the wake-up bell sounded and the usual morning activities had begun before leaving the orchard. Once doors were unlocked and windows thrust open, joggers had started their before-breakfast run, and the grounds people were working on the campus, it was easy for them to blend into the busy scene.

Carrie returned to the dorm exuberant and sped down the hall to her room. Ginger was getting dressed, and Kim was sitting on Carrie's bed, biting her nails. They both let out a whoop when Carrie burst into the room and slammed the door shut.

"Thank goodness you're here," Kim cried, clapping her hands.

"Ditto!" Ginger said. "Even I was worried."

"Did everything go okay?" Kim asked.

"It was fantastic, once I got by Mr. Oslo."

Kim unconsciously began biting her little fingernail. "He saw you?"

"Just missed."

"Tell us about it," Ginger said, wide-eyed.

Then Carrie regaled them with all the details.

"You weren't at all scared," Kim commented when she was finished.

"I didn't say that," Carrie said. "But I can honestly tell you it was the most exciting thing I've ever done."

"I'm just glad it's over," Kim sighed.

"You were terrific, Kim, especially 'cause I know how you felt."

"What'll you do for an encore?" Ginger asked.

"I'll think of something," Carrie said, laughing.

"Let's go have breakfast," Kim groaned. "I've had enough excitement to last me a lifetime!"

The next couple of weeks were relatively calm. Kim was pleased that Carrie didn't come up with any madcap schemes to beat the system, and the two of them kept to their work schedules and played at the appropriate time. It was understood that Carrie would see Mark whenever possible, and often they made a foursome with Kim and whomever she happened to be going out with.

One Saturday night after they returned from a movie and Frost Bite date, the girls sat downstairs in the lounge and talked about the evening. Kim confided in Carrie that she never thought she'd want a steady boyfriend, but after seeing Carrie with Mark, she was beginning to think she might change her mind.

"You mean you like Mark?" Carrie asked.

"Of course I like Mark but not that way. I think he's just perfect for you, and I hope someday I find Mr. Wonderful."

"You will," Carrie assured her. "For a long time I had no one, remember?"

"How could I forget?" Then Kim added thoughtfully, "Sometimes I think you're beginning to sound like me."

"And sometimes I think you're beginning to sound like me."

"I think that in biology that's known as a symbiotic relationship—a close association of two different organisms that benefit each other."

"That sounds like something I would say," Carrie said, and then the two of them had a fit of the giggles.

As Christmas vacation approached, everyone was busier than usual. Besides studying for finals and finishing papers, there were cards to send and presents to buy. An additional thrill for Carrie and Kim was the prospect of becoming full-fledged members of The Club.

They hardly thought about the initiation rite—Renée had said it would be a breeze—and mainly concentrated on the party. They volunteered to be on the decorating committee, which required enormous ingenuity. It was impossible to do anything in advance for fear of creating suspicion. After a lot of brainstorming, Carrie and Kim came up with the plan of decorating the secret meeting place with balloons and crepe paper. The balloons could be blown up once they arrived at the party, and the rolls of crepe paper could be taped to the walls at the last minute. Everyone congratulated them for their idea, and Carrie and Kim were more confident than ever of being made senior members.

On the Sunday before the celebration, Kim was invited to a combination horseback ride and picnic. She went with the understanding that she would return to the dorm by two-thirty in order to do her homework. Kim was still haunted by the terror of letting a good time jeopardize her scholarship, and no amount of coaxing could make her change her mind.

It had been an especially strenuous ride, led by one of the more macho students, and Kim wasn't too unhappy that she had to leave early. The dorm was almost empty when she returned. The few girls who were there were closeted in their rooms, studying for finals. Kim looked forward to the luxury of a hot, uninterrupted shower. At that hour, no one would be waiting around for her to finish, and she could take her time.

Kim shed her riding clothes, wrapped herself in a towel, grabbed her soap and shampoo, and headed for the bathroom. She chose the shower stall at the farthest end because it was near the window and had the most light. Then she hung her towel on the door, and was about to turn on the faucet when she heard the door open. There was a moment of silence and then Renée's familiar voice, "The coast is clear, Ellen. We can talk."

Kim was surprised that they would choose the Ellsworth bathroom for a conversation, but like her, they probably thought privacy was guaranteed at this odd hour. She was about to ignore them and reached for the knob when Ellen asked, "What time should we begin the hazing on Tuesday?"

Kim was riveted by the word "hazing," and couldn't help listening for more.

"Midnight," Renée answered. "We'll have the four girls meet us at the dock ten minutes before twelve and they can begin the swim across the lake right away."

"This is the best idea we've come up with yet for an initiation," Ellen said enthusiastically.

"I think so, too. It's really original—a midnight swim in

December. Maybe this should become a tradition for The Club."

"I can't imagine finding anything to surpass it."

Kim was shocked by what she was hearing. She and Carrie had taken for granted that the initiation rite would be tame. This was nothing like what they'd anticipated. It was bad enough to expect four girls to break curfew, but it was sheer madness to ask them to swim across the lake in the winter. The temperature could be below forty degrees, and with the wind-chill factor it would feel like the Arctic. The darkness meant they might get disoriented and lose their sense of direction. If anyone saw some suspicious activity on the lake, and reported it to the authorities, they'd be expelled.

Kim acted instinctively. She wrapped herself in her towel and flung open the door of the stall.

"You must be crazy," she cried, stepping onto the tiled floor. "You'll never get me to swim across the lake in the middle of the winter."

Renée and Ellen, who were leaning against the sink, looked at Kim as though she were an alien monster.

"What are you doing here, Kim?" Renée's voice was shrill.

"I was about to take a shower. Fortunately I hadn't turned on the water or I never would have heard you."

"You're not supposed to be in on our plans," Ellen barked.

"I couldn't help hearing you, but I'm glad I did. There's no way you're going to get me into that lake in December."

"Listen, Kim, why don't we pretend none of this has happened. Secrecy about the initiation is its main feature. Just go along with us, don't tell the others, and we'll forget all about this." Renée was trying to be conciliatory.

"But I'm not going through with it, no matter what."

"If you hadn't been eavesdropping, you wouldn't have had time to worry about it." Ellen could sound awfully menacing.

"I've got news for you, Ellen," Kim said bravely. "If I found out at the last minute that I was required to swim across the lake, I would have balked. That would have created worse problems."

"This means you won't be a member of The Club," Renée warned. "You'll be the first junior member in S.N.'s history who hasn't joined."

"I'm sorry about that, but I can't help it. This is just too dangerous."

"You're chicken, I guess," Ellen said. "I never would have thought so."

"I think it's stupid, Ellen, and you can't convince me otherwise."

"Well, if you're that adamant, there's not much we can do," Renée said resignedly, "but I trust you won't scare off anyone else."

"I have to tell Carrie. I got her into this."

"You don't have to," Ellen said.

"You don't understand. I'm responsible for getting her interested in the first place."

"Kim, I can't believe this is you talking. I had you figured all wrong."

"You just don't know me, Renée. I'm loyal to my friend."

"What about loyalty to The Club?"

"I think The Club is making a mistake. You're asking us to do something that's life-threatening."

Renée, who tried to remain calm, was rattled by the implication. "We're doing something that has a certain element of risk, but I wouldn't call it life-threatening."

"You are being dramatic," Ellen said.

"Look, you two, I'm not going to be part of this, and if I know Carrie, she'll have the brains to refuse, too."

"You're hopeless," Renée sighed.

"We might as well go. She's not going to change her mind," Ellen said.

"I'm sorry about the whole thing," Kim said as she watched them leave.

"I bet you are," Ellen said sarcastically before following Renée out the door and slamming it shut.

Kim was dejected as she went back into the shower and turned the faucet on full blast. The spray pounded down on her, but no amount of soap and water could wash away her sadness. The last thing she wanted to do was alienate Renée and Ellen and give up The Club. But even if she was proved wrong, Kim knew she had to follow her instincts.

Chapter 13

*K*im, still unnerved, returned to her room after her shower, put on some clean jeans and her most comfortable sweatshirt, plunked herself down at her desk, and attacked her math homework. She spent ten minutes poring over the first problem, one of those brain teasers that ordinarily she found challenging, but her mind wouldn't work. She couldn't stop thinking about the incident in the bathroom and wanted desperately to talk to Carrie. She needed her best friend to unburden herself to, and also to warn her about the hazing.

Kim knew Carrie was seeing Mark and wouldn't be home until five o'clock. That meant ninety minutes of agonized waiting. She decided there was no point in studying, and to make the time pass she would do something totally mindless. There was a TV in the lounge, and the movie buffs would be glued to some Sunday afternoon film. Joining them would be a distraction, so she went downstairs and unobtrusively slid into an empty chair in the back of the darkened room.

More than a dozen kids were so engrossed in the old Woody Allen film, periodically cracking up, that they didn't notice her. It was just as well, because Woody's antics didn't interest her in the least. Still, it was better than being alone in her room, and she forced herself to stay until the end.

When it was over she ambled up the stairs and strolled down the hall to Carrie's room with the idea of leaving her a note saying how urgent it was that she see her. The door was half open. Kim barged in, and was so surprised to see Carrie that she screamed, "What are you doing here?"

Carrie was taking a jacket out of her closet. "I live here, remember?" she said, laughing.

Kim carefully closed the door, breathed heavily, and leaned against it.

"What's wrong with you?" Carrie asked.

"Something's happened," Kim answered.

"Can it wait? I was getting a jacket because Mark wants to give me a Frisbee lesson and it's getting cold out."

"It can't wait." Kim slouched toward the bed and sank down.

"What's it about?" Carrie had one arm in the sleeve of the jacket.

"It's about you."

"About me?"

"Not just you. It's about me, too . . . and The Club."

"It's about us, you're saying, and The Club." Carrie tried to be patient.

"We can't go through with it."

"What are you talking about, Kim?"

"I heard Renée and Ellen talking about the initiation. They expect us to swim across the lake next Tuesday at midnight!"

"What's so bad about that?" Carrie was working on her zipper.

"Did I hear you right?" Kim said.

"I said what's so bad about that."

"Are you kidding? Bad isn't the word for it! It's the dumbest thing I ever heard of. We can drown, or freeze to death, or get cardiac arrest."

Carrie forced a smile and shook her head. "It's no big deal. We can both swim."

"Neither of us have swum all year. We're not exactly in Olympic shape."

"We don't have to break any records, just get across the lake."

"You mean you'll do it?"

"Of course. Won't you?"

"No way . . . and neither should you."

"Look, Kim, you talked me into joining The Club, and you were right. Now you're telling me to get out."

"Because I don't want you to do anything so stupid. I'm not going to let you."

"You don't own me, you know." There was an edge to Carrie's voice that Kim had never heard before.

"Of course not, but I feel responsible for you."

"Or maybe you just want to control me."

"I want to protect you, Carrie. Like you said, I talked you into S.N., and now I feel responsible for what they make you do."

"Do me a favor, Kim, and butt out. I'm capable of making my own decisions."

"Even if it means getting pneumonia?"

"You can't scare me with that argument. If it'd been up to you, I never would have met Mark in the orchard."

"That wasn't nearly as dangerous. All that could happen then was you'd get caught. This could kill you!"

Carrie looked at Kim as though she had flipped out, and she didn't bother to respond to that last remark. She simply said, "If you don't mind, I have to leave. Mark's waiting for me."

Then she strode out of the room and left Kim still slouched on the bed.

For a few minutes Kim was too stunned to move. She tried to make sense of what had just happened and wondered if she'd been too bossy and forced Carrie to overreact. Whatever the reason, she knew Carrie was inflexible.

Kim tried desperately to think how she could stop her. One way would be to report the hazing to the headmistress. But that would destroy The Club and betray the members, something she could never bring herself to do. Then Kim decided that the only person who could reach Carrie was Mark. She knew she could swear him to secrecy, The Club's existence would not be revealed, and her best friend would be spared an unnecessary ordeal.

Kim mapped out her strategy. She would call Mark at five-thirty. By then he would be back in his dorm and they could have a private conversation. She returned to her room feeling a little better now that she had a plan of action.

Nancy was there and remarked how much she enjoyed the Woody Allen movie. Then she said, "I didn't expect to see you there. I thought you were studying."

"Got bored," Kim said, shying away from the truth.

"That's my old roommate. For a while there, I thought you were turning into a grind."

"Not me," Kim said, trying to keep up her end of the conversation.

"I'm glad to hear that. All work and no play . . ."

"I know, I know."

"In that case, how about a game of Ping-Pong right now?"

"I'd like that," Kim lied. She wasn't sure if she had the strength to hold a paddle, but there was no point in inviting a lot of questions.

They went down to the Ping-Pong room, where a doubles game was going on.

"We're just warming up," one of the players said. "Do you want to come back?"

"We'll wait," Nancy said. "It looks like it'll be a good match. Okay, Kim?"

"Sure," Kim said. She really didn't mind because she thought there was plenty of time. But she didn't realize how long it would last. The score was 20–20, and one team had to win by two consecutive points. It didn't look like that would ever happen. At five o'clock the game was still going on.

Nancy was getting into it, applauding and yelping after each point. Kim managed to fake her enthusiasm, but she was getting twitchy. If she didn't reach Mark before dinner, she might not get him until Monday. Then there wouldn't be much time for him to work on Carrie.

Finally, there was a service ace, followed by a spectacular smash, and the game was over. The players were exhausted but elated. Before the teams left, there were handshakes all around, promises for a return match, and low bows to Nancy and Kim for being such a good audience.

Then Kim and Nancy started warming up, but Kim was anxious about the time and cut the preliminaries short. She and Nancy were evenly matched and usually the games were close. Today was different. Kim's concentration was off and she kept slyly glancing at her watch, worried that she wouldn't reach Mark. She was so jumpy that she played recklessly, and Nancy won easily, 21–10.

"Are you feeling okay?" Nancy asked.

"I'm fine, just not coordinated today, I guess."

"You want a return?"

"No thanks. I've got to make a phone call."

A look of annoyance clouded Nancy's face. "Why did you bother, then?"

"Sorry, Nance. I forgot about it. . . . I mean, I thought we'd start earlier. . . . I mean, finish sooner."

"Okay, okay. I'll see you back in the room." Nancy could never stay annoyed with her roommate for long, and wandered out.

Kim hurried to the private phone room, grateful that it was unoccupied. She reached Mark's dorm without any problem, and a lethargic voice said, "I'll try tracking him down."

Kim was about to leap out of her skin. She did some deep-breathing exercises that she'd been told in her phys. ed. class was supposed to allay anxiety. It didn't seem to help, so she tried some T.M., transcendental meditation, which she'd read in a magazine could distance one's mind from immediate problems. That was equally ineffective, and she was about to start chewing her nails when she heard Mark saying, "Hello."

"Thank goodness, Mark," Kim cried, "you're there."

"Who is this?" Mark asked.

"It's me, Kim. I have to tell you something, but you must promise not to tell anyone else."

"If I can," Mark said.

"It's about Carrie."

"What about her? You sound as though something terrible has happened."

"It might if you don't stop her."

"Kim, tell me. I'll do anything." Mark couldn't keep the alarm out of his voice.

Kim stuck her head out the door, made sure no one was around, and then proceeded to tell Mark all about The Club and the hazing. The last thing she said was, "You're the only one she'll listen to, Mark."

"You were right to tell me, Kim. And I agree with you, it's very dangerous."

"Then you'll talk to her?"

"I'll call her right now."

"Good, Mark. You're our only hope."

"I'll do what I can."

Kim went to her room and told Nancy she wasn't feeling at all hungry. "That picnic lunch must have poisoned me," she said.

"Should I bring you something?"

"No thanks. I'll just skip dinner."

"Why can't I ever do that? I'm always famished."

Kim was relieved that Nancy left for the dining room without asking any more questions. While she was gone, Kim paced up and down, imagining the conversation Mark was having with Carrie. In the beginning Carrie would be resistant, giving all the arguments she'd presented earlier to Kim. But Mark would be very persuasive, and soon she'd see how foolhardy the whole thing was.

Kim went through the scenario several times in her mind, and had almost convinced herself that everything would be all right, when Carrie stormed into the room. Her face was red, and her eyes flashed angrily. "How could you?" she roared. "Not only did you betray The Club, but you went behind my back, to *my* boyfriend, to report on me. There's only one word to describe you, Kim, and that's 'fink.'"

"Carrie, I had to. It was the only way. Mark will never tell anyone else."

"That's not the point. I don't like you interfering in my life."

"All I hoped for was that you'd listen to him and . . ."

"I did listen, and I'm convinced you gave him a very distorted version of what's going to happen."

"I just reported to him what I heard. I can see why you'd be mad at me, but I was only trying to accomplish one thing."

"For your information, the one thing you accomplished was to get me into a fight with Mark!"

"That's the last thing I wanted to have happen."

Carrie's eyes narrowed. "I'm beginning to wonder about you," she said, and then slammed out of the room.

Chapter 14

*F*or the next two days there was a frost between Kim and Carrie that was almost visible. They took great pains to avoid each other in the classroom, the dining hall, and the dorm.

Kim was more downhearted than she had ever been in her life. Her good intentions had backfired. Short of going to the authorities, she felt she had done everything in her power to deter Carrie from being victimized by an ill-advised ritual. All she had succeeded in doing was alienating Carrie and causing her to have a major argument with her boyfriend. There was no point in talking to Mark again. Kim sensed that his conversation with Carrie had only hardened her position.

Kim went through the motions of going to class, responding to questions, socializing with her friends. But all she could think about was the swim. In spite of an inner voice that said, "Beware, you've done enough damage," she had to see firsthand what was going to happen the night of the initiation.

Since she was no longer included in The Club's plans of getting the initiates out of their houses, she was totally on her own. And not only did she have to slip out the window without anyone's help and make her way to the lake undetected, she had the additional problem of not being seen by the S.N. members. If they caught her spying, they might get the wrong idea and force her to return to the dorm.

Knowing the timetable helped. She would arrive at the lake five minutes before everyone else and hide in the bushes. Also, she had sweated out Carrie's rendezvous with Mark, and knew what precautions to take.

On Tuesday night, Kim laid out her dark clothes and sneakers and left the door ajar so that she could sneak out without disturbing Nancy. There was no problem about Kim waking up, because she was too nervous to sleep. At eleven-fifteen she crawled out of bed, took off her nightshirt and stuffed it under the pillow, grabbed her clothes, and went into the hall to dress.

Then she ran down the stairs and into the first floor bathroom. It was a chilly night, and she was aware of the danger of Mrs. Gore being awakened by a cold draft. Therefore, she opened the window as little as possible, slithered through, balanced herself on the ledge, and jumped.

The night was eerily silent and the moon cast ominous shadows. Kim knew she must hover close to the buildings and watch for signs of Mr. Oslo. She was practically on top of the guardhouse when she saw him about twenty feet away, puffing on his pipe and talking to someone. Whoever it was must have been allowed on the campus, because Kim heard a low murmur of conversation and an occasional chuckle.

Kim quietly opened the gate, passed through, and had the presence of mind to close it behind her. Then she sped toward the lake and found a clump of bushes where she could hide. She sank down on the ground, trembling with fear. The combination of breaking the rules with no support system and anticipating the disaster that might befall Carrie, Jennifer, and Pam was awesome. A stiff breeze was coming from the lake, and the idea of wearing only a bathing suit made Kim shudder even more.

She didn't have too much time to speculate, for suddenly there was a flurry of activity at the edge of the lake. A rowboat had approached the shore, someone was climbing into it, and then there were three distinct splashes. The test had begun.

Kim eased herself away from the bushes and inched as inconspicuously as possible toward the shoreline. She was heartened by the fact that a rowboat was accompanying the girls, undoubtedly manned by Renée and Ellen.

They were halfway across the lake and Kim was beginning to feel calmer when one of the swimmers wailed, "I can't make it. Help me. Help!"

"Okay, okay," Renée said.

"I'm going under!"

Kim recognized Jennifer's voice.

"Be quiet and tread water," Ellen instructed.

Renée vigorously rowed toward her. There was a mad scramble, the boat tipped precariously, and then Kim could see Jennifer had managed to climb aboard.

"I'm freezing," she muttered.

"Here's a towel," Renée said. "You'll be fine."

"I hope so," Jennifer said. Then she added, "Sorry to be such a wimp."

"At least you tried," Renée said.

Kim was sure that remark was referring to her. Probably the others had been told she had chickened out and Renée was using her as a bad example. Still, Kim was convinced she'd made the right decision, and this was reinforced when less than two minutes later Pam cried, "My legs are numb. I can't swim anymore!" There was a note of hysteria in her voice.

"We'll pull you in, Pam. Save your energy and float on your back," Ellen said. Then she ordered Renée to pull harder on the port side.

Kim could just make out what was happening: Renée deftly rowed the boat next to Pam; Ellen seized her hand and turned her around; then with Jennifer's help they grasped her under the armpits and lugged her over the gunwale.

Kim's mouth was dry with fear. Jennifer and Pam were safe, but what about Carrie? She was still plowing her way across the lake. Kim was tempted to scream, "Give up, Carrie, give up!" But the way things were between them, she suspected that might have the exactly opposite effect.

It was getting increasingly difficult for Kim to see, but she had to know Carrie's fate. The only way was to get nearer to the boys' dock. Her heart was pounding, but without a second thought, she raced to the opposite side of the lake and ducked into the boathouse.

She gasped when she saw someone silhouetted against the window. Whoever it was spun around and saw her. There was no point in running away, Kim thought. I'm too tired to run fast and I'll be caught.

The figure took a tentative step toward her, and a soft but distinctly male voice asked, "Kim, is that you?"

"Mark . . . Mark," she breathed, and ran toward him.

For several seconds they clutched each other for emotional support. Then they moved toward the window and peered out.

"Why doesn't she give up?" Kim asked desperately.

Mark shook his head. "I don't know," he said in despair. "I don't know."

Carrie was slowing down, and Renée and Ellen

whispered words of encouragement. It was obvious that her strength had been sapped.

"You're almost there," Renée said. "You can do it!"

Carrie's arms were flailing ineffectively. The more she struggled, the less headway she made.

"Kick your feet, Carrie. Kick your feet!" Ellen said urgently.

Carrie did just that, and in one superhuman burst of energy, she miraculously covered the last fifteen yards. Then she clung to the dock while the rowboat swung to the side and Ellen jumped out. She helped her up the ladder, and wrapped her in a towel.

"Congratulations," Ellen said. "You're terrific!"

"Fantastic!" "Super!" "I don't know how you did it!" the others chimed in.

Carrie stood there, shivering and speechless, a vacant look on her face.

"We've got to get back," Renée said. "Pile in."

Kim had thrown her arms around Mark in a victory hug. "She did it! She did it!"

"I can't believe it. For a while there . . ."

"Don't say it. I was thinking the same thing."

Then, not wanting to do anything stupid like burst into tears in front of Mark, she said, "I've got to get back before they do. I'm sure they've arranged for someone to unlock the door to the dorm. My problem is to get by Mr. Oslo."

"I have just the thing—my computer pass. You can use it."

"What about you?"

"The guard knows me. I don't have to worry."

"Mark, you're a lifesaver."

"There's a lot of that going on tonight," he said with a touch of bitterness.

Chapter 15

*O*nce Kim was safely back in her own bed, she gave into the tears that had been so close to the surface for so long. The past forty-eight hours had been a nightmare, and now it was over. Still, there were repercussions she would have to face. Because of the stand she had taken about the initiation, she would be a social outcast among The Club members. But worst of all, Carrie must hate her. Kim cried herself to sleep, wondering if she would ever recover from the loss of their friendship.

It was little more than an hour later that Kim was startled from her deep sleep by loud voices. Kim thought she must be dreaming, but the noise persisted and then she heard the words. "Something happened to Carrie." "She was rushed to the hospital." "An ambulance came."

Kim, exhausted and confused, shook her head and tried to understand what she was hearing. She repeated the words, "Carrie . . . ambulance . . . hospital," and she knew something terrible had happened.

"Oh no!" she screamed, and leapt out of bed.

"What's going on?" Nancy mumbled.

"Don't know," Kim said, and bolted into the hall.

Nancy staggered after her toward a group of girls huddled together.

"What happened?" Kim asked hoarsely.

"It's Carrie," Ginger said. "She woke up in the middle of the night, shivering and burning up with fever. I knew she needed a doctor. I told her I'd get our housemother, but she insisted on going to Mrs. Gore's room herself. She seemed half-crazed, kind of delirious, so I thought I'd better not argue. Instead, I followed right behind her because I wasn't sure she could make it."

"Did she?" Nancy asked.

"Barely. She stumbled into Mrs. Gore's room and then fell down on the floor."

"Oh no," Kim groaned. "Poor Carrie."

"What happened then?" someone asked.

"I take back everything I ever said about Mrs. Gore, because she knew exactly what to do. She called the ambulance from General Hospital, and in less than five minutes it was here. They took her out on a stretcher. It was awful."

Kim's knees turned to jelly, just listening to the story, but she knew this was not the time to fall apart. She had to get to the hospital to see Carrie.

"I'm going to the hospital," Kim announced.

"We're not supposed to," Ginger said. "Mrs. Gore went with her in the ambulance, and I wanted to meet her there, but she said the hospital wouldn't appreciate an invasion."

"I don't care," Kim said, thinking she'd broken so many rules that night, one more wouldn't matter.

Then she zipped into the room and slid into the clothes she'd dumped on the floor less than two hours earlier.

"Is there anything I can do?" Nancy asked.

"Pray," Kim said, grabbed her bag, and flew out.

The first thing she did was call a taxi and arrange to have it meet her outside the gate. Then she telephoned Mark, forgetting what an ungodly hour it was to call the dorm. Kim hadn't anticipated the operator giving her such a hard time, but she finally convinced her that it was an emergency and got through to him.

"What's wrong?" Mark asked, not bothering to say hello.

"It's Carrie. She's in General Hospital—chills, and fever, and passing out."

"I'll go there," Mark said, and slammed down the phone, too upset to be polite.

Kim understood perfectly, because he'd reacted just the way she had. Nothing could stop her now. In the excitement, the front door had been unlocked, so she had no trouble leaving. Then she ran boldly across the campus to the gatehouse.

Mr. Oslo, who must have been responsible for directing the ambulance to Ellsworth, was leaning down, talking to the cabdriver through the open window.

"My friend's in the hospital. I must go see her," Kim said.

"I understand," Mr. Oslo said, and helped her climb in. "Good luck, young lady."

"Please hurry, driver," Kim said as he revved up the motor. "My friend . . . she could be . . ." Kim couldn't finish the sentence.

"I'll do the best I can."

Then he took off at breakneck speed and in less than seven minutes they arrived at the hospital entrance. Kim flung a five-dollar bill at him, scrambled out of the taxi, and slammed through the revolving door.

"Carrie Gordon . . . what room?" she asked an elderly woman at the reception desk.

"She an emergency?"

"Yes, tonight."

The receptionist took forever looking through some forms that were on her desk. Finally she said, "Room 207, second floor," she pointed to the elevator.

Kim was too impatient to wait for the elevator, and bounded up the stairs, two at a time. When she opened the door to the second floor, she literally bumped into a nurse.

"Sorry," Kim said. "I'm looking for Carrie Gordon in 207."

"I'm sorry," the white, starched nurse said stiffly. "You must go to the waiting room. These aren't exactly visiting hours."

"Please, she's my friend. She needs me."

"I'll see," the nurse said, softening a little. "Depends on the doctor. The waiting room is at the end of the corridor on the left."

"Thank you," Kim said.

Kim went down the dead-quiet hall and wished her stomach would stop churning. She was astounded when she saw Mark was already there but at once she felt better. He jumped up and led her to the couch where he'd been sitting.

"How'd you get here so fast?" she asked.

"I've been helping my science teacher on a special project. He's got a car, and he owed me a favor. He let me borrow it."

"What about Carrie?"

"The doctor's with her now."

"And where's Mrs. Gore?"

"She's gone off to make some phone calls. Probably calling Carrie's father."

Mark looked grim, and Kim had to bite her lip to keep

from bursting into tears. The two sat in silence, deep in their own thoughts, until a middle-aged, bespectacled woman, a stethoscope hanging around her neck, approached them.

"You're Carrie's friends?" she asked.

"Yes," they answered in unison.

"I think Carrie would like to see you. But only one at a time and don't stay more than five minutes. She's in the first room past the nurses' station."

"Thank you, doctor," Kim said. Then she turned to Mark. "You go first."

"No, you go, please," Mark said. "I want to be by myself for a few minutes."

Kim knew he wasn't just being polite, so she took a deep breath, stood up, and as steadily as possible walked down the hall to 207.

Kim entered the room timorously, and was so shaken by the sight of Carrie that she couldn't speak. Her face was deathly pale and a tube was attached to her arm for intravenous feeding. Kim walked over to the bed and sat down beside her.

Carrie managed a weak smile and said, "I've got pneumonia, like you said."

"You'll be okay, right?"

Carrie nodded her head. "I was really dumb. I should have listened to you."

"I'm just glad you're alive."

"You're still my best friend?"

"You know it!"

"Lying here, I realized how much I care about our friendship . . . more than I could ever care about The Club."

"Now you have both."

"No way. S.N. means nothing to me if you're not in it. It's all silly and I took it so seriously. On the way back in the boat, Renée said that the rule was anyone who made it halfway across the lake could be a member. I think they make up the rules as they go along. I feel like such a fool. I practically killed myself and . . ."

The tears started to stream down her face, and Kim handed her some tissues from the night table. Kim was also on the verge of tears, but she willed herself to be strong. She took a comb out of her pocket and made an attempt to run it through Carrie's hair.

"Mark's outside and you don't want to look like . . ."

". . . like I just swam the English Channel."

They both began laughing and crying at the same time, a relief from the unspeakable tension.

"You're something else," Kim said softly.

"No, you are," Carrie murmured. Then she grasped Kim's hand and squeezed it, and the two friends smiled silently at each other. There was nothing else either one of them had to say.

ABOUT THE AUTHOR

Patricia Aks was born and raised in Detroit, Michigan. She attended Sarah Lawrence College and Wheaton, where she majored in English literature, and received an M.A. in Educational Psychology from New York University. She has worked as an editor and a writer. Her most recent book for Fawcett was *The Real Me*. Ms. Aks is the mother of two children and lives with her husband in New York City.